ISBN the3percenters edition 9781916425309

Cover design by Tom Taheny Graphics, Galway

SINS

SINS

New Irish Crime Stories

the3percenters

Edited by Ferdia Mac Anna

About the Authors

the3percenters is an authors' collective and publishing partnership formed to promote emerging writers. The group were originally associated with the annual Dalkey Creates Writing Festival.

CONTENTS

The Welfare Visitor   *Martin Keating*   1

A Casual Killing   *Jenny Wright*   9

The Lust of Lavinia   *Mark Bastow*   30

Rhythm of the Sea   *Adrian Taheny*   54

The Snake that Ate its Own Heart   *Alix Moore*   69

My Law, Not Your Law   *Mark Bastow*   98

Vainglorious Bastard   *Caroline Bale*   115

Doppelganger   *Martin Keating*   136

The Apology   *Adrian Taheny*   152

Let the Punishment Fit the Crime   *Alix Moore*   171

Itch   *Susan Rodgers*   188

Biographies   218

There is no calamity greater than lavish desires. There is no greater guilt than discontent. And there is no greater disaster than greed.

~Lao Tzu

The Welfare Visitor

Martin Keating

Bill had parked the car facing away from the house, and, as he talked on the phone, Laura kept watch through the rear-view mirror. When he finished the call, he said they'd best wait until the woman was alone: her partner was unpredictable and wouldn't welcome the visit.

Bill smoked, while Laura checked and rechecked the list on her clipboard.

'Nervous?' Bill asked.

'I don't like confrontations,' Laura said.

'Who does? Oh, here we go.'

A bulky shaven-headed man came through the front door of the house, hobbling on a crutch and holding his jacket in the other hand. He leaned against the gate pillar to put on the jacket and limped the last few steps to the white van slewed against the kerb.

'Hunker down,' Bill said, and Laura did so, as the van pulled out and drove past.

'Wait a mo.' The second hand swept a few rotations across the face of Bill's watch. 'And, five, four, three, two, one. Go! Good luck.'

Laura brushed her tweed suit and adjusted her watch and bracelet. She took a last glance in the mirror, plucking off her diamond earrings and dropping them in the coin tray between the seats. 'The details, Laura,' she scolded herself.

Walking down the footpath, she coughed to clear her throat and practised saying, 'Hello, I'm Laura.'

The front door had a long crack in one of the panels,

as if someone had taken an axe to it. The living room window had a starfish-shaped fracture in the bottom corner, repaired with duct tape. 'Shit,' Laura muttered. Her reflection didn't have the ID card hanging from a lanyard. She'd removed it when they'd stopped for coffee, and now she dived into her bag to recover it.

A thin blonde woman with a suspicious look on her face answered the doorbell. She opened the door a little way but left it on the safety chain.

'Hello,' Laura said. 'I'm the welfare visitor. My name is Laura.'

'Uhm,' said the woman.

'You are Noleen Burroughs?'

'Shouldn't I have got a letter?'

'Yes, you should.' Laura handed her a photocopy through the gap in the doorway.

'Mail goes all over the place here,' the woman complained, 'no one gives a shit.' Her hand had an egg-sized bruise just above the wrist. 'My partner's not here'— she handed back the letter— 'and he doesn't want people in the house when he's out.'

'This is just a quick check on things, Noleen. You're on my schedule for this morning.'

'Now is not a good time.'

Laura said, 'I can't make appointments. It's policy not to. Visitors have been robbed ...' She let her voice fall, '... and worse.'

'Look, I'm sorry, but I can't let you in. All right?'

'Well, I'm sorry too, but I'll have to put this down as denied access. That will suspend payments until the assessment can be completed.' Laura half-turned, as if to go.

'Stop the money?' the blonde asked. 'Couldn't you say there was no answer?'

'I have to tell the truth, Noleen. You came to the door

2

and you wouldn't let me in. It could be three months before you're scheduled for another visit.'

The door opened fully. The blonde woman gripped her sides and tugged at her lip with her teeth.

Laura inclined her eyes towards the livid bruise on the woman's arm. 'Won't it upset your partner more if the money is stopped? It's only a few questions, I look at the family's accommodation, and then I'm done. Barely more time than we've already spent talking.'

'You can't go around the place on your own. I gotta be with you.'

'Fine,' Laura said.

The woman stood to one side. Before going in, Laura ran her finger down the damaged door panel and tapped her pen at the cracked window. She made notes on the clipboard and took out her camera phone.

'Have the council sent anyone?'

Noleen had a crescent and star tattooed on her cheek. 'I've been in,' she said. 'Went in with the baby to the housing services. They don't give a shit.'

'I'm making notes of this, Noleen. I'll follow it up.' Laura took a photo of a long beard of green scum that hung down from a broken gutter connection.

'Is there mould inside?'

'All upstairs. The doctor's warned us not to let the baby get asthma.'

'Can you show me the cooking and washing facilities, and can I see out the back?'

Noleen showed her the cooker with only two working rings, the leaking refrigerator, and the stains on the wall and the ceiling from the broken extractor. Click, click. Laura took more photographs.

'Washing machine?'

'That works, most of the time.'

Laura opened the drum and looked inside. 'That seal is

3

just about perished,' she said.

Noleen led her into the back yard. On the grass, by the rotary line, there was a playpen containing a fat unruly baby.

'That's my Usain.'

'How old is the little man?' Laura made a wide-eyed face at the baby. He scowled back. 'Is he walking yet?'

Noleen crouched down and the child waddled unsteadily towards her. 'He's a lazy lump, like his old man. And he likes to eat, like his old man. You tore up mummy's titties, didn't ooh, and didn't ooh?' Laura saw a tattoo of a genie on the woman's lower back as Noleen reached her finger into the playpen to tickle her son.

Laura looked in the rubbish bins. Looked at the drain coverings. Looked up at the rear gutters. Noleen pointed. 'The gutter back here is cracked since we moved in.'

Click, click. Laura made notes. Laura asked questions.

'Partner's name?'

'Thomas.'

'What does he do?'

'What does anyone do around here?' A wry smile. 'He signs on, that's what he does.'

In the front room, there was a flat-screen television, a cable box, a couple of games consoles and a music centre.

Laura's attention was caught by the two photographs on the mantelpiece. One picture showed a laughing ogre brandishing a bowie knife while holding Noleen in a headlock.

'That's my Thomas', said Noleen proudly.

In the other photograph, Thomas held a large fish towards the camera.

Laura photographed the fat brown stain in the corner of the ceiling.

'Have you had much problems with the plumbing?' Laura asked as they went upstairs and into the bathroom.

'Stuff gets stuck.' Noleen said. She flushed the toilet twice. 'That's what you have to do to get rid of a load. As for thinking you could put a jam rag down there, forget it.' The rich got a better draw on their jacks, she complained; stuff was just thrown together for the poor.

While they were talking, Laura's phone rang. She held up a finger and stepped onto the landing.

'Twenty-minute call,' Bill said. 'Anything?'

'I'm upstairs now; it shouldn't take much longer.'

'I'll ring the house number in ten minutes then.'

'That'll be great,' Laura said. To Noleen, she said, 'Boss man. We are so monitored.'

'At least you have a job,' Noleen replied grudgingly. 'As for us, we can fucking starve.'

Laura photographed the brown tracks from the bath taps to the plug hole.

'Can I see the baby's accommodation?'

She looked at the small box room, cluttered with toys and stuffed animals. She tutted at the damp stain running all along the front edge of the ceiling.

'Isn't it a disgrace, though?' said Noleen at her shoulder.

'Are you able to keep the baby's clothes dry? What about the hot press?' She saw something flicker in Noleen's eyes.

'That's all fine,' Noleen said, putting herself between Laura and the landing. 'No complaints there,' she said. 'It's about the only thing that works in this house.'

'Great,' said Laura, making three ticks on her clipboard. 'Attic?' she asked.

'I wouldn't go up there,' Noleen shivered. 'It's like Paddington station for rats.'

Laura made more notes, asked about other pests. She said she'd like to go back into the bathroom and take off the bath panel. 'You've rats down here as well.' Laura pointed to the bullet-shaped droppings. 'I'll put you down for a visit from pest control.'

'Jesus, that fucker, Tom, told me the noise was silverfish.'

As Noleen leaned in, their heads touched. Backing away, Laura heard the downstairs phone ring.

'Jesus,' said Noleen. 'What if it's him? What do I say?'

'I'll talk to him if you want,' Laura offered.

'No, no, you stay here. Stay right here and don't budge.'

When she heard Noleen's faint 'Hello?' from the living room below, Laura slipped off her shoes and tiptoed to the hot press. Keeping her eyes on the living room door, she slid a hand into the press and began to feel around.

'She's here at the moment,' she heard Noleen say downstairs. Bill was obviously pretending to be Laura's supervisor. 'No, she's not in the room with me.'

Then Noleen pushed the living room door shut—Bill would be asking her to answer some confidential questions about the visit—and Laura risked putting her head into the hot press.

She ran her fingers over the clothes, pressing and feeling around the sides. She probed and reached, feeling sweat on her shoulders and back. Bingo! The package, fat as a salami, foil-covered and in her hand. Then she was in the bathroom again, stepping into her shoes with her prize secure in the zippered middle compartment of her bag.

She was waiting at the bottom of the stairs, consulting her clipboard, when Noleen came out of the living room. 'Was that your partner?' she asked.

'Nobody. A wrong number.'

'A supervisor may ring you, about the visit.'

'Is that right?' said Noleen, rubbing her neck.

'Is there anything you want to tell me, that I haven't asked?'

Laura made herself go through the questionnaire, looking at the pencil marks she had made. To get Noleen's attention and keep her downstairs, she asked if she could have a glass of water. She drank it by the sink looking out at the back garden.

Two magpies were perched on the playpen, watching the baby with interest. Seeing them Noleen ran to the door, shouting. The magpies flew to the boundary wall, and she picked the baby up out of the playpen and brought him in.

'The fuckers steal his rusks and peck him,' she said, showing Laura the scabs on the top of the baby's head.

'I'll put them on the pest control list too.' Laura took a photograph of the marauding birds.

'Goodbye, Noleen,' she said at the door. 'See, it didn't take long after all.'

'Goodbye, Usain.' She tickled the baby's cheek, and he tried to bite her finger.

Laura's knees shook as she walked up the road to the car. As they drove out of the estate, the white van passed them coming back. 'Oh, shit, shit.' Nausea hit her. She bent over, putting her head between her knees and sucking air in.

Bill chuckled. 'That was a close squeak.' He drove one-handed while holding the foil package. He tossed it and caught it and said, 'That's a good weight.' He gave it back to her and tousled her hair. 'OK, babe?'

'Oh, Jesus,' she said. Her cheeks felt clammy to the touch. Grey worms squirmed in front of her eyes. She straightened up and opened the window. 'Jesus Christ.'

Bill reached over and took the lanyard and identity card from around her neck, flipping them out the open window. 'Won't need that again. Good job, good job.'

They got to the slip road and he powered up the incline to the motorway. 'Fucking brilliant.' He glanced over his shoulder, looking for a gap in traffic he could squeeze into.

'He's going to kill her,' Laura said.

'No, he won't,' said Bill. 'If anyone's for the chop, it's him. Better them than us, I say.'

'Shit,' said Laura.

Bill started whistling. He swept into the fast lane and gunned the engine.

'It's shaping up to be a cracking afternoon.' He laughed. 'What do you think? Get a bit of distance in and then turn off someplace. Have a drink in a beer garden and kick back. Candy from a baby, eh?

A Casual Killing

Jenny Wright

At first, Helena thought it was a car alarm. Or was the storm getting stronger? As the wailing became louder and louder, she realised it was approaching sirens sounding above the uproar of the winds. They couldn't be coming here, surely? It was too soon. She'd only just killed him and there had been no noise—had there?

Fred had simply gaped at her after the first blow, his eyes glazing over by the fourth or fifth—she couldn't remember. A Roald Dahl story sprang to mind, where the woman who had killed her husband first cooked and then fed the murder weapon, a frozen leg of lamb, to the investigating officers. Well, she couldn't feed a hammer to the police, could she? How to dump it? She'd need to be sharp about it, no dilly-dallying, hammers don't disappear by themselves.

I know. I'll put his fingerprints on it; that's what they do on the telly—make it look like suicide. No, that wouldn't do. If he were going to kill himself, it would be hard to argue that a hammer would be his weapon of self-destruction.

She hadn't absolutely hated Fred. She would even go so far as to say she was, occasionally, quite fond of him. But, on balance, he'd had to go, one way or another. A man in his fifties, and not the new fifty either; the old fifty: paunchy, balding and 'fond of a drop', he had recently adopted an alarming new dress code, which she heard him refer to as 'hip', alerting her conclusively that something was afoot. She'd been nagging him for years about his sloppy appearance and now suddenly he was listening? He must have known that a bottle of Armani eau de toilette on the bathroom shelf would not go unnoticed—she'd always hated 'man perfume'. Probably to disguise the smell of Bianca, his personal assistant, who was liberally doused in something cheap.

She had met Bianca, of course; Fred had introduced them and by the time it took to say 'hello', she knew there was something between them. She and Bianca had nothing to say to each other. *Despite our common interest*, Helena thought.

Bianca affected a few unfortunate verbal tics: 'Oh, don't mind lickle me,' she was heard to say, more than once, under the illusion that it made her cute and vulnerable. She also tended to refer to herself in the third person as in: 'Bianca is not a happy bunny', which was unforgiveable in ways too many to mention, although Helena gave it a try to much hilarity amongst her friends.

Fred's sudden fondness for vegetables and salads also gave Helena pause for thought. Once, she caught him standing sideways in front of the hallway mirror and sucking in his gut. She was amused that he had not realised that adopting all these new habits was a cliché. 'A pretty heinous crime, in my book,' as she, no stranger to cliché herself, had told her friends. Whatever the reason, there was no doubt that it spelled 'affair', though that word might have elevated whatever it was the two were having to a more respectable level than they deserved.

No need to ask what *she* saw in him. Bianca, real name, probably, Doris, was very late thirties, with bosoms that may well have been enhanced and auburn hair with only slightly perceptible roots.

Whenever Helena had occasion to meet Bianca at parties, she recognised the greed. She could see her eyes darting around the place as though totting up the worth of every piece of furniture, every clock, every knife and fork. *And probably getting the sum wrong*, Helena decided.

At a dinner party in the house of a wealthy colleague of Fred's, where art covered every inch of the walls, Bianca, staring at a Paul Klee, was heard to ask, 'How much would that go for?' in an unfortunately sudden moment of quiet. Helena was very pleased to see the look of distaste on the other guests' faces before they continued with their conversations, dismissing Bianca to the 'not like us' category.

'She really thinks Fred's going to leave me for her,' she told her friends. "She's going to be a much better wife. She won't neglect him by going out to work. She'll stay at home and give him the kids he says he wants. She won't let herself go. Well, not until she's been married to him for a few months and loses the will to live.' This was all discussed at length in the pub after many vodkas had slipped down, and they were all screaming with mirth.

Early on in their days together, Helena had supported Fred financially while he did his master's degree in Business Administration, which had allowed him the opportunity to make large amounts of money over the years. His wealth had not escaped Bianca's notice. Helena was damned if she was going to hand him over without a fight, just when he was seriously minted.

The final straw, however, was the cessation of smoking. In all their years of marriage, he'd smoked like a chimney. Now, suddenly, he had stopped, causing him to be even more irritable than even Helena could have believed possible.

A combination of circumstances had prompted the hammer incident. He barked at her once too often and she snapped. When he walked in after work that day, she had not planned to kill him at all. *Though, Lord knows, I've had reason over the years.* It just happened on the spur of the moment and, no doubt, if she had had to go searching for a weapon, she might have thought better of it in the time it took her to find something suitable with which to do him in. She surely would not have selected a hammer, if she'd had a choice, but it was just so *handy*. In the crime novels she favoured, women who chose to kill used poison. It seemed somehow less violent, but, of course, the outcome was still death. She had briefly considered it in moments of extreme fury but discarded the idea. Really, she should just have left him, but that would have led to all manner of battles over property, with which, frankly, she could not be bothered.

She and Fred lived together in a well-practised state of passive–aggressive hostility, driven by a general spirit of non-cooperation. They expressed this in a number of creative ways, such as turning radiators on and off, opening and closing windows and changing the location of all kitchen implements. She greatly enjoyed watching Fred search for the spatula, which she had relocated to the third drawer down, whilst he, on the other hand, took much pleasure in watching her having to turn the kitchen radiator back on over and over again, as he harrumphed about the cost of fuel. Sometimes, she relayed these tales to her friends, all of whom had their own marriage, or rather war, stories, of course, and causing endless hilarity amongst the group, which Fred called her 'coven'.

But they'd never come to blows before tonight.

He'd come in from work to find her in paint-spattered overalls and bath cap—not a pretty sight, she would admit—a cigarette in one hand, a gin and tonic in the other, admiring the sage green walls she had just finished painting. At an earlier time in their marriage, he might have found this eccentric attire quite charming. Tonight, however, putting his briefcase down on the hall table, he looked over at her with a sneer. Normally, he would say nothing, but it was the cigarette in her hand that pushed him beyond the limits of tolerance. She blew the smoke in his direction and smirked. If she'd just handed him the cigarette, he might have held his tongue.

'For the love of Christ, woman, have you taken leave of your senses? Look at yourself in the mirror?' The disgust on his face was more maddening than the words he spat out.

Rage surged up from her belly, increasing in intensity till she felt her face boiling. She put her cigarette out calmly in the ashtray and placed the gin and tonic on the small table, upon which lay the hammer. She picked it up and applied it forcefully to the side of Fred's head, several times.

When she had finished, she stood back to gaze down on her handiwork. The rage was subsiding now to a slow simmer, tinged with annoyance at the further mess that she now needed to clear up.

Quick! Think, think, think. Were the sirens coming her way? If so, who had alerted the emergency services and why? If they were not heading to her, she had time to clean up, hide his body, hide the hammer. No, it was a lot more complicated than it had at first seemed.

Earlier on, killing him had presented itself as an obvious solution to the problem. Of course, he wasn't expecting it. Indeed, when she had time to reflect later, her clearest memory was the surprised look on his face after the first blow. She had nearly stopped to spell out the problems with their marriage to him at that moment. They'd been married for twenty years, and she'd done a lot of muttering under her breath. Occasionally, she'd gone in for a bit of shouting, especially in the early days, when there was hope.

He never listened to her complaints. 'Women are always complaining. There's nothing to be done about it; they're never happy,' he was wont to grumble, regularly.

'Perish the thought you might listen to what I'm

saying,' she would reply, also regularly.

Of course, it wouldn't take the police long to find the culprit. It didn't help that she frequently voiced her frustration with him and had often threatened to kill him. In a jokey kind of a way. Not quite so jokey, of course, as it now turned out.

Bearing all that in mind, she didn't think she could get out of this. Some of her friends had heard her saying she'd like to kill him on numerous occasions, but, then again, some of them made the same threats about their own husbands. Obviously, it was exaggeration, and not to be taken seriously.

One Christmas, he came home far too late to help with a dinner party he had persuaded her to throw and after some of the guests had arrived.

'Oh,' she said, 'there you are, at last. I was just saying I was going to kill you.'

'I'd prefer you not to make death threats, at least not in public,' he had replied. How they all laughed.

Then there was that time when one of their little venom-swapping spats got out of hand in front of their friends. That night, moments after they arrived at the pub, it was discovered that each had supposed the other to be the designated driver. Both were utterly outraged to discover they may not be able to have more than one drink. It had quickly descended into a full-blown domestic, and she had thrown a pint in his face. No one was laughing that time. She had completely lost her temper, and they withdrew in disarray, still shouting at each other, leaving a stunned silence in their wake. For a minute or two, the remaining customers turned to their drinks with exaggerated concentration, till someone sniggered and a roar of conversation engulfed the pub, providing the gathering with renewed energy. It had taken them months to go back to that pub, and they never went there together again. Helena was furious with herself for allowing her true nature to reveal itself. Up to now, only her husband and her family had been witness to the real Helena.

She supposed she could plead insanity—plenty of her friends and family might attest to that—but then she'd be locked in an asylum, which did not seem any more attractive a prospect than jail.

The sirens seemed to stop some distance away. She looked down to see her clothes covered in blood. Ripping off the overalls and bath hat, she frantically cast around for somewhere to hide them. The stove! She'd lit it to help dry the paint. It was worth a try. The hat melted instantly and then burned with a roar, igniting the overalls. She picked up the hammer, wildly looking around for somewhere to conceal it. Even in her panic, she realised that although the handle would go up in flames, there was the matter of the metal head, which clearly would not.

'Maybe the sirens aren't coming here,' she hoped for a brief moment.

Her hopes were dashed, however, by a loud banging at the door. She opened it, forgetting the bloody hammer in her hand. Bianca! It was difficult to know who was the more shocked.

'It's you!' Helena said. What the hell was she doing here? 'Here,' she shouted, 'Quick, take this.' Bianca looked at her blankly, as though she did not recognise her, and grasped the proffered hammer.

Helena pushed past the bewildered woman, slamming the door, and raced out into the stormy night. Panic set in and she bolted up the street towards the main road. It took about ten seconds for the rain to soak her through, and a very bedraggled woman was seen running in the middle of the road, cars avoiding her but not stopping. 'She looked too mad,' they told reporters when news of the murder trickled through the grapevine to the local media that night and arrived as an avalanche in the national news in the morning.

Eventually, Helena came to a halt under a tree to catch her breath and attempted to order her thoughts. Discovered by Bianca! How bizarre! Drenched and shocked, she realised there was no getting out of this. She considered, briefly, that she might just keep running, but the life of a fugitive did not hold much appeal. Besides, she was standing under a tree that afforded little shelter and whose branches were flailing around so vigorously, that she feared for her safety.

She slowly made her way back to the apartment to face the music. She was shivering now, and her only concern was to get warm and dry. Her thoughts were swirling around in her head so rapidly that none lodged for longer than a nanosecond. She kept going back to Bianca's arrival. What was she doing there? She'd never appeared at the flat before. And tonight!

She still had not come up with any kind of plan when she arrived at the front entrance of the apartment block to see Bianca being led away to a waiting squad car by a policewoman. What? The stern demeanour of the police officer alerted her to the fact that Bianca was being taken against her will. That and the fact that she was saying over and over—as though repetition would make her story more credible—that she had only just arrived and that it was his wife who had killed Fred.

Just then, Bianca spotted a very dishevelled Helena and, pointing at her, bellowed, 'That's her. She's the one!'

The stony-faced policewoman showed little interest in what Bianca was saying. Instead, she urged her forcefully into the squad car as another officer approached Helena, cautiously.

Helena summed up the situation: Bianca was being arrested. She had been found with the body, probably still holding the hammer. The police were showing her no sympathy, whereas, they were being kind to Helena and informed her of her husband's death in gentle tones.

On the journey to the station, alone in the back of another squad car, Helena formulated a plan, her resolve considerably stiffened by the inkling that she might get out of this if she played her cards right. It did not take much to extend the shivering and shaking from the soaking she had received to appear as though the news of Fred's death caused her to lose control. She did a bit of wailing in the car. By the time they reached their destination she was in full control of herself.

Wrapped in a blanket and sipping weak tea from a polystyrene cup, she told the officers that she had rushed out the door and down the street, turning back in time to see Bianca scurrying through the front entrance. Her husband had confessed to an affair with Bianca, and she had left the house suddenly in anguish. Warming to her theme, she sobbed, 'But he swore he'd broken it off with her. He said she was taking it really badly.' Here, Helena upped her game and whispered, 'He said he was terrified of what she might do,' and the sobbing increased.

Inwardly, she snorted in derision at the detectives' tactics—she was far too cool by this time to make any mistakes when they asked her over and over again to repeat her tale, which varied not a jot. It seemed as if their hearts were not really in the interrogation: they showed her sympathy, offering to refill her cup of tea and asking if she wanted breaks in the questioning.

~

The prosecution seemed happy to pursue Bianca as the principal suspect and were disposed to believe Helena's version of events, the reason for which became clear at Bianca's trial.

Several months later, Helena found herself in court, as a witness and victim. She'd often imagined herself in the witness stand, but it was the divorce court she had had in mind. She had even rehearsed her testimony of Fred's ill-treatment and had portrayed herself as hapless victim of mental cruelty by a man who controlled her by keeping her short of money, which was patent nonsense as her job paid her handsomely. But she had not yet refined her divorce case to her satisfaction. Luckily events had taken over; Fred was gone, and here she was at Bianca's murder trial.

Bianca was tried on two counts: murder and conspiracy to commit murder. On hearing the charges, Helena was mystified. She still did not know why they had pursued Bianca and not her. They accepted without demur that her fingerprints were on the hammer because she had been using it to hang a picture on the newly painted walls. The police had not believed Bianca when she said that Helena had thrust it into her hand. And what conspiracy?

It turned out that Bianca's real name was Earthstar. *Earthstar?* Helena thought, *that wouldn't have been my first bet.* As soon as she was old enough, Helena learned, Earthstar had unburdened herself of both her name and the alternative parents—by whom she was deeply embarrassed and whom she had not contacted in years. As Bianca, she invented a new set of fictional parents, who lived in the Home Counties and voted Tory—probably Brexit too. She boasted about them, believing these new versions boosted her social standing. When an older couple—he with a straggling beard and she, wearing a long patchwork dress, both reeking of patchouli—turned up in court to witness their daughter's murder trial, she did not acknowledge them. Bianca was still ashamed of them, despite her current circumstances.

The poor old things, Helena thought, *being responsible for* that.

In the witness box, clutching an expressly purchased, tiny hanky, with which to dab her eyes from time to judicious time, Helena gave her evidence. Holding onto the front of the witness box, as though too weak to support herself in her anguish, she repeated the story of Fred's betrayal and subsequent confession shortly before the appearance of Bianca that terrible day, with many embellishments and dramatic outbursts of emotion. With every telling of this tale, she managed additional pathos. She faltered and looked down at her hands. The prosecutor asked her if she needed a moment. 'No, no, I'm fine,' she whispered and bravely continued.

'He begged my forgiveness,' she stammered. 'Fred swore it was completely over and he was so very, very sorry, and he had loved me all along.' Fred had added that he was frightened of telling Bianca. She was very volatile, and he did not know what she might do. She was looking straight at Bianca as she dropped this pearl. Bianca did not return her look, but, instead, stared down at her hands.

Bianca's defence counsel did not give Helena an easy run.

'Is it not the case that you had withdrawn from the marriage years ago and that your husband had to take comfort where he could?'

'I loved him with all my heart,' she sobbed, 'even after he … after *she*'—and here she looked over at Bianca—'*she* tried to take him away from me.'

'Oh, I see, so you knew they were having an affair before the night of the murder?'

'No, of course not,' Helena protested, 'but it was obvious something was going on, and he was quite mean to me'—by which she meant her audience to infer 'unspeakably cruel'. She played a very convincing wronged wife.

'I suggest that you became enraged when he told you

about his affair with Miss Pettystone, and you picked up the hammer and killed him—in a Fit of Jealous Rage!' The barrister's voice rose dramatically with this thrust.

Nearly right. At least, about the rage and the hammer, Helena thought and marvelled that the learned counsel had used the phrase without irony.

'No, no, no,' she pleaded, 'I adored him.'

The barrister went on in this vein, but he was not up to her icy calm in the line of fire.

She was devastated; she loved Fred so much and was running out in deep distress after his confession when Miss Pettystone had arrived at the flat, just as she was leaving. Here Helena began to weep again, glancing at the jury to see if they were buying it. As one, they were turned towards her, their faces bathed in compassion. *God, I really am good at this,* she thought.

Though not permitted to speak—by her lawyer, Helena presumed—it was obvious that Bianca's mood lurched between downcast and enraged, in equal measure. She muttered to herself from time to time and glared at her adversary. She was clearly riding a wave of righteous indignation, which did not endear her to the jury. *No* acting talent, Helena crowed to herself.

Other witnesses had come forward, lured by the limelight. A man who had seen her battling through the rain could only give an approximate time, within about ten minutes, for his sighting of Helena—which was fortunate, but not for Bianca. The pathologist could not be more time-specific either. As the motorist gave his evidence, Helena could not help noticing how fit he was. 'Another time,' she said to herself.

It was only in court that she heard a neighbour testifying that she had heard a prolonged howl coming from the adjacent flat and dialled the emergency services. At first, she had not recognised the sound as human and it took her a minute or two, she said, to realise it was a woman howling. The time of her call was recorded, but since the time of Bianca's arrival was not, it was assumed to be her making the noise. Helena had not actually been able to recall 'the event' as the lawyers sensitively described the murder, but she supposed it must have been her screaming.

At first, not privy to the prosecution's case, she was surprised and a little put out when the text messages between Bianca and Fred were read out in court. She was also momentarily amused, not least because it had taken him ages to master the art of texting when he first agreed to have a mobile phone. Some of the texts put her in a very poor light, in court, for everyone to hear. For example, her husband referred to her, his wife, as 'the boot'. As in: THE BOOT GOING TO COVEN TONIGHT. He even developed the witch theme with BLACK AND MIDNIGHT HAGS, in another. Quite humiliating. It put Fred in a worse light, of course, and Bianca's replies included the words OLD BAG and WITCH, which did not remotely help her case.

At first, the texts concerned Fred's leaving her for Bianca. There was much lovey-dovey cooing and kissing in these texts:

CANT WAIT TO MEET YOU AT YOUR FLAT, or ONLY ONE MORE DAY TILL BOOT GOES TO TENERIFE AND WE CAN BE ALONE!

Very brave, she thought. He'd never have said it in her presence, but in the privacy of his own mind and his phone, he was released from her authority. To be fair, Helena thought, he probably really did think he was going to leave me, but never managed to muster enough nerve to tell me. I can just see him rehearsing in the mirror.

However, as a plot to do away with her began to develop. Helena could not believe her luck. So *that's* why the police didn't pursue me, she thought. She gasped when the texts made it clear that they were going to murder her that very day. She was genuinely incensed, momentarily. She had to plumb the depths of her determination, then, not to smirk when the plot became clear, and the diminutive hanky just barely served to conceal a smug little smile, after the initial outrage had passed. What a delicious coincidence! She could not have prayed for better evidence against Bianca.

The erstwhile Earthstar had arrived at the appointed time to help Fred dispose of Helena's body. He had recently purchased a very sharp knife—they knew that they would not be able to use one from the set of knives in the stand in the kitchen; how to explain its disappearance?—and Bianca was to come over with her car. Together they would carry Helena's body, wrapped in a carpet, to the boot of the car. They too had been watching crime programmes on the telly. Nothing could possibly go wrong.

Unfortunately, neither of them had been watching telly closely enough. They had failed to understand that texts could be recalled, amongst other lacunae in their knowledge of criminal investigations. They seemed to believe that deleting their texts was security enough. A rookie mistake, Helena sneered to herself. He was remarkably dim-witted for someone so successful. In any event, the police found the knife and even the receipt in Fred's wallet. Bianca claimed ignorance, but it was all there in the deleted texts.

Helena's statement was the only proof that Fred had dumped Bianca: hearsay, in other words. There were no texts to that effect, which was strange considering the large number of texts between them. But, the combination of Helena's stellar performance in court, a lacklustre defence lawyer without imagination, the texts, of course, and, not least, the jury's dislike, conspired against Bianca and the verdict came back 'guilty'.

The contents of the texts between Fred and Bianca were what really damned her, as it turned out. In describing their marriage to Bianca in one of his lengthy texts, Fred said he'd given his wife everything she could possibly want and still she seemed ungrateful.

Helena was incredulous. *I bet he really believed he was the bountiful husband, and I bet Bianca believed that she was a more worthy recipient of his munificence.* But she could not believe that her wimp of a husband would have the balls to carry through such a plan, even if encouraged by Bianca, about whom she had no such doubts. There was a hard glitter to the other woman. Helena had once caught her staring at a set of pearls she was wearing at a do, Bianca's eyes then flitting to the matching bracelet, and taking in the rings Helena was wearing. She had thought Bianca was actually going to ask if they were real pearls, her calculator at work again. The woman never looked anyone in the eye, except Fred, into whose eyes she gazed longingly when she thought no one was looking and laughed coyly at his pathetic jokes all the time, so much so that Helena felt sick. She had wanted Helena's life, to replace her, Helena now realised.

Bianca's parents were hanging on to one another and gaping, as the evidence against their daughter piled up and the verdict was returned.

'She's rejected everything, everything we ever stood for; not only rejected but embraced a consumerist, not to say hedonistic lifestyle,' her mother told the journalists who dogged them both after the case. One paper even suggested that the stark conditions of her upbringing had determined Bianca's future course in life and made her resolve never to return to the poverty of her childhood, 'by fair means or foul', thereby suggesting that killing her lover's wife was the route she chose to realise her dream of a better life. They had not seen her in years, her parents confirmed, and had hardly recognised her at first. 'She's had a boob job,' her mother finally whispered in a tone of disbelief mixed with disapproval. They looked even more dishevelled and bewildered as they left the court. They did not reappear for the sentencing and, as far as Helena ever knew, did not visit their daughter in prison during her life sentence.

As for Helena herself, she soon tired of living in their old flat in their old town. Her friends had believed her protestations of innocence at first and had turned up to support her with enthusiasm and many bottles of wine. But Helena carried on as though nothing had happened and, indeed, acquired quite a new spring in her step. She found it difficult to conceal the triumph of her performance in court and she let her guard down. They found Helena's constant reflections on Bianca's character distasteful and downright mean. They hoped for some expression of regret or sadness in Helena's demeanour, but found only glee.

One of them asked her once if she missed Fred at all. 'What's to miss?' she fired back, before collecting herself and launching into an unconvincing litany of his good points and how she missed him.

Once one of them tentatively voiced her suspicions, it was like letting out the bath water. It turned out Helena had a lot more character flaws than they had previously allowed for and, one by one, they stopped seeing her. This, she found unforgiveable, since they used to roar raucously at every tale of Fred's misdeeds and even encouraged her in her excesses. But she was comforted by the fact that, although they admitted their suspicions to each other, they were still completely flummoxed as to how she got away with it. And, of course, they never stopped talking about it after that, ever.

Given her propensity for outspokenness, Helena had also managed to fall out with all three of her sisters, who now never wanted to speak to her again, mainly due to her constant criticism of everything in their lives, but particularly their choice of husbands. Neither did she hold back on passing judgement on their offspring—two of whom were called Lysander and Ophelia—names that drew new levels of derision from Helena. To the last sister to keep in contact, recently divorced for the second time, she had even suggested that she might find another man, if she were to frequent dimly lit bars, where the lighting might be low enough, and men might look at her with drink-induced rose-tinted glasses. This was not well received, and all contact ceased forthwith.

No, Helena rarely thought about Fred and the past. As part of her self-reinvention, she moved to London and enrolled at drama school. While concocting a convincing curriculum vitae, she wished she could insert her court performance as her best and most successful work. As an encore, she had honed her acting skills while answering the door to the incessant gaggle of journalists who doorstepped her for days after the sentencing. To one particularly persistent reporter, she grandly announced, 'I forgive Bianca,' which was used in the headline the following day. Helena hoped Bianca would see it. She missed the attention when the press decamped to a fresher, more gruesome crime scene.

Her audition, though, confirmed her talent and she was accepted. She reclaimed her maiden name, wondering what had possessed her to change it to Fred's in the first place.

She loved her time at the school and, on her graduation, although there were not that many parts for women of her years. Nevertheless, there was the odd one, including Martha in *Who's Afraid of Virginia Woolf*, which might have been written for Helena.

Touring the country with a repertory company, with a week or two in each town, suited her. When they were booked for a week in her own hometown, she developed a prudent dose of flu and an understudy took over. The understudy was quite happy with the new arrangement, but the audience contained a few very disappointed members. Some of her former friends and family had booked seats out of morbid curiosity. The air of gleeful expectation turned to dust when the announcement was made that Helena's part was to be played by someone else. Her sisters actually left before the first act began. Despite the fact they weren't speaking to her, they were all dying to see her on stage, nevertheless.

Helena enjoyed a decent lifestyle with her acting money. Well, that and Fred's life insurance, which was eventually paid to her after Bianca's conviction. Due to her elevated financial status, she was not desperate for work, which afforded her the benefit of being very relaxed at auditions. This gave her enormous advantage over her penurious peers and kept her more or less continuously working. She took taxis to rehearsals and, wishing her fellow actors to think she was as broke as they were, asked to be dropped off out of sight of the theatre.

She got used to her life in London and very pleasant it was too. She bought a flat with a pool in the basement and luxuriated in her new-found wealth and freedom. *How very clever of Fred to have such brilliant insurance cover*—and she momentarily thought of him fondly. However, although she quite liked male companionship from time to time, the odd drink or dinner, on balance, she preferred her own company, and thought it wise not to marry again. She'd served her sentence.

She had a few friends from the theatre, but it suited her that those friendships were always short-lived and only lasted the duration of a play, in spite of many must-keep-in-touch conversations and exchanges of phone numbers, which she just deleted. Although they went out together sometimes and had great evenings in the pub on their nights off, she never got to know them more than superficially; she skipped over her past without any detail, and, in that particular milieu, they were not that interested anyway. She was happy, she realised, for the first time in her life. Most of all she was liberated. No husband, no family. Why had it taken her this long to work out that she needed to be alone? All in all, she reflected, she'd done the right thing.

Then, one day, glancing dreamily at a news channel on her phone, she saw something that made her sit up. A banner headline proclaimed: BIANCA DUNNIT! She read on. Bianca had 'found God' in prison and confessed to the murder of Fred. She wanted to offer her heartfelt apologies to the 'poor widow of my victim'.

Helena felt a chill. What the hell was Bianca playing at? At rehearsal that day, she could not remember one line of her part. She claimed migraine and left. Her thoughts were jumbled and incoherent, and she could not come up with any reason for Bianca's confession. Later though, with the benefit of a stiff brandy and some more reading, she realised that confessing her crime— or admitting to a crime she did not commit—would certainly mean an earlier release. Helena had not considered what might happen when Bianca was released, and for the first time since the day she killed Fred, her confidence was shaken. She was worried.

It took Bianca a further two years to gain her release, but Helena never slept easily again. Becoming increasingly anxious as time went on, she was deemed unreliable due to frequent absences, and acting parts ran dry. She spent most of her time at home now.

Answering a ring on her doorbell one day, Helena saw Bianca staring straight into the security camera, a faint smile on her lips and a steely look in her eye. For the first time, Helena suddenly thought she might have met her match. She was almost relieved to see her; she'd been worrying about it for so long.

Bianca spoke, still looking intently into the camera. 'Hello, Helena.'

Lust is a strong tower of mischief and hath in it many defenders, as neediness, anger, paleness, discord, love and longing.

~Diogenes

The Lust of Lavinia

Mark Bastow

The adult world was the greatest disappointment that a girl could suffer. Lavinia almost felt like stepping back into her girlhood and returning to Mumsy's eight-bed hideaway down at the end of Minori Avenue in Dalkey.

After considering her plight at some length in Tankers Wine Bar, she ruled it out. She had to face up to this thing called 'the world' and take it on squarely. Be resolute as every woman should be. Face adversity.

Her main adversity at this moment was a man: a man that went by the name of Mr John Maddison. He had sexually harassed her on her first day at work. What else would you call making her spend a whole day photocopying but sexual harassment? It was to humiliate her into being a submissive sex slave. She just imagined Mr John Madison dribbling all over her while he humped her as she was trapped in that small space between the photocopier and the stationary cupboard.

In her mind the sensations of revulsion and delight swirled and quickly evaporated when Gorgeous George, the owner of Tankers, asked her if there was anything else he could do for her. Oh, there certainly was, but George's partner, Hectic Henry, was keeping an eye on proceedings from the bar.

Her first night in her own little place in Sorrento Drive. Wasn't it exciting? No, it wasn't. It was quiet. Even with the telly turned up, it was silent. The emptiness crowded her in. The furniture and furnishings were delightful and stylish. Nothing boring. Nothing cheap.

Everything had class. Ten out of ten to Mumsy for doing such a good job. But an empty house was an empty house, and a house without people was an empty house no matter how well furnished it was.

She had already phoned her old classmates. They were all too busy to spend time with her. They always were. Her evenings were free all week apart from her Thursday nights at Mr Matsumoto's aikido class. Daddy had insisted on the lessons if she was to leave home. A girl needed to be able to defend her honour. Whether or not she cared to defend her honour was then a question of choice he said in that man-of-the-world way.

Mumsy was right, she should have got a cat for company. Then she thought how it would sound to her friends. I brought a cat for company. *Did you hear that?* Poor Lavinia brought a cat for company. What a sad soul she is. She is lonely. The only company she could get was a cat.

Her mobile tinkled to the sound of running water— her mobile greeting of the week.

'Yes, Mumsy, I'm home, and I am just about to put one of your cottage pies from the freezer into the microwave and let it ping away. Oh yes, I'm so happy. Thank Daddy for buying the house and a million trillion thanks to you for decorating and furnishing it. You have such style. I must have such style as well for appreciating it. Oh, thank you, Mumsy, for saying so. Yes, work was so exciting. I did so many different things it was so interesting. You what, Mumsy? You think John Madison is a hunk? No, I won't telly Daddy. No, I wouldn't want you to miss the new soap. *Amalfi Way*, is it? Set in the Rialto district of Dublin. Bye-bye, Mumsy. Love to Daddy. Love to Bertie the cat.

Lavinia sat down and had a little weep. Providing you did it at the right time, weeping was good for you. You should do it to relieve stress, show others how beastly they were and at other appropriate times. It was best to practise it occasionally and keep the tear ducts in tip-top condition. Sometimes tears were the best response, even when you felt more like breathing fire.

Then she had an idea. Sex. She would have sex. Christen the bed.

She rang Chris. 'Sorry, Lavvy, but I'm up in Belfast at Queen's.'

Rang James. 'Wow! Didn't know you were available. I am with someone now. OK to ring you another time when I'm free? Yes?'

Rang Liam. 'Supper and breakfast? I'll be right round.'

~

Liam was such a disappointment. His conversation was poor. His foreplay was rushed. The main event was over so quick, poor Lavinia came nowhere near an orgasm. Hopefully there would be a second act. She fell asleep. She woke up with him fumbling on top of her.

'Not now.' She tried to push him off.

He insisted. It was a limp performance.

'You woke me for that?'

'Most women appreciate my prowess.'

'Do they?'

'Yes, they do!'

Breakfast in the Corner Note was the highlight of their encounter. Her French toast was the most. Liam expected her to pay. She looked at him in disbelief. She told the waiter that her friend would pay. Liam had to pay. He grumbled. Then, outside he tried to kiss her. Smudge her make-up? Think again. Was he better than a cat? Possibly.

She agreed to walk down to Coliemore Harbour with him. He was telling her how lucky she was to have him. He would forget about her grumpiness in the night. She would build up the stamina at sex once they had been together for a few months. Under his coaching, her performance would improve. The cheek of it! There was nothing wrong with her performance. It was him. She wondered why she had invited him over the night before. Then she remembered Chris and James were both unavailable and Liam was the substitute.

Then, he had the cheek to say he wanted a key to her little place. Why? Of course, he needed a key if he was going to move in. Move in! Forget it Mr Flopsy. Then he said she obviously needed a man in her life, and he would ignore her protestations. He said she was just getting emotional. Believe me by this time, she could easily have got emotional. Then he started on about what she would cook him for supper! He didn't really mind as long it wasn't shellfish.

They walked along the stone pier in silence. His mobile rang. He fumbled. The phone tumbled down the steps. He went down two of the steps and bent down to pick it up.

She kept remembering him saying *her* performance would improve under his coaching. Indeed! She would teach him. As he was still bending down, she pushed him.

Goodbye, Mr Flopsy!

It all went horribly wrong for a moment. Liam regained his balance, grabbed her wrist and pulled her to him, holding her tight from behind.

Now what did Mr Matsumoto say about being grabbed from behind? That's it. Bend the knees, wrist lock and throw. Let's try. Wow! It worked. Down he went and over the side.

Splosh, into the water.

Her first thought was to run away before an angry Liam emerged from the water, but she couldn't resist looking. Where was he?

He didn't surface. Should she dive in? No way. *It took me ages to get my make-up right today. Would I ruin my Jaeger two-piece by jumping into salt water?* She looked at her watch and waited five minutes. Still no sign of him. Too late now to do anything.

Over a million people worldwide die of drowning every year and that limp prick has just joined them. Served him right. Should have learnt to swim. Then on reflection she smiled. Mr Matsumoto would be pleased with me. I never did that move so well in class. She felt quite exhilarated and sexed-up. What she needed now was a *real* man.

~

Lavinia walked to work. Madison's Solicitors was only ten minutes away up by the Dart Station. Mr John Madison was in the office kitchen. She remembered her mother's description of John as hunky. Lavinia looked at him afresh. With livestock, you always look first at the whole beast, and then hone in on the details. Good large frame. Good set. Good lean carcass. Firm hind quarters. Nice hands. Handsome face. Good teeth. Good breeding material. On reflection, Mumsy was right. John was a hunk. John was a *real* man.

'Thank you, John, I'll have a black coffee. No, believe me I am sweet enough.'

'I'm sorry to ask you, Lavinia, after all the photocopying and scanning yesterday. Would you mind doing some shredding?'

'Not at all, John. Anything you want.'

'Have you used a shredder before? You do know how to use one?'

'No. Could you show me?' Her big eyes looked up at him.

Into the photocopying room they went. He demonstrated.

'Can you please show me again which button I press?'

'Certainly. Look there are only two buttons. One, on. One, off. It is this one for on and this one for off,' he said pointing at the buttons in turn.

'This one for on, and this one for off, Mr Madison?' Lavinia said, purposely pointing at the wrong buttons with a giggle.

'No, the buttons are the other way around. See this button is green. Green is for on. The other button is red. Red is always off. Do you understand now?'

John was laughing at this stage. She flicked her hair. She had sprayed some perfume into it in the cloakroom. The flick released a swath of scent. It was a little seduction trick Mumsy had taught her.

'Yes. I do know now. This one for on and this one for off. You explain it so well. Have you always been good with machines?'

'I suppose I have always been interested in machines. One of my hobbies is restoring steam engines.'

'That is so interesting. Are they working engines?'

'They are when I have repaired them.'

'Wow! Tell me what types of steam engines they are.'

'All types. I mainly repair engines for model boats, model railways. My own collection is of model static traction engines and pumps.'

'You mean pumps, like for pumping water?'

'Yes.'

'That is *so* fascinating.'

'You really think so?'

'I do. I do so admire someone who is good at engines. You're an engineer of the miniature.'

'Thank you for saying that. I suppose I am. "An engineer of the miniature." I rather like that. Now do you remember which button is which?'

'Yes. I will always know which button to press. Thanks for being patient with me.'

'It's getting a bit hot in here,' he said wiping his brow.

She smiled. She had glanced down at his trousers. He was getting excited. It wasn't a question of if—it was a question of when she would bed him. Pity about that ring on his finger, but, as Mumsy says, challenges are there to be overcome.

As she emerged from the photocopying room, Lavinia noticed that the Office Secretary, Sheila Duffy, gave her a dirty look.

~

That evening, Lavinia had an idea. The surrogate family. That was what Daddy said was the appeal of the soaps. The soaps provided surrogate families to people who didn't have a family of their own or whose family wasn't very interesting. Lavinia thought that at this new stage of her life, she didn't have a family, so she would get her own surrogate family by watching this new soap.

Well, what a disappointment her new family was. None of the characters appealed to her. They were nauseatingly successful professionals with degrees and high-flying jobs. Lavinia went for the tear bucket. Here was she, an unsuccessful poorly paid photocopier operative.

She channel-hopped. The soaps held no appeal. Current affairs were of no interest. As for the documentary channels, who on earth wants to know about the feeding habits of whales or the development of the jet engine?

Then she chanced on a porn channel, and then on another and another. Now *these* she found interesting. After watching porn channels for three hours, she was exhausted and confused. How on earth do you find such good-looking men and, more importantly, men who could do it for so long? Dalkey and Blackrock men didn't have stamina like that. Would she have to go to the Northside?

One of Lavinia's many qualities was decisiveness. At that moment, she decided to venture into the Northside. When to venture? She would venture after work the following day.

She slept well. Jumped out of bed. Got ready. While she was eating her natural yoghurt, she reflected how right Mumsy had been about Mr John Madison. He was a hunk, and if he'd been bonking Mrs Madison for five years, he had probably developed considerable endurance in that department. He would probably be glad of someone new to shag. She would still make her visit to the fabled Northside, but if it didn't live up to its reputation, Mr John Madison was a definite candidate. She picked out a little red minidress.

Most of that day she spent helping Robert Doyle—the other solicitor in the practice. Poor Robert didn't score so highly as John in Lavinia's livestock judging. He wouldn't get a rosette, but she was very pleased that his eyes were always straying over to her legs. It was a great investment that Millie Mackintosh dress. Cheapest item in her wardrobe, but it had great pulling power.

After work, she walked out of Madisons Solicitors and over to the Dart Station. She got off at Dublin Connolly and went in search of randy Northsiders. She made a beeline for the Tambourine Bar. She positioned herself on a high stool by the bar where she could watch everyone who entered. Her friend, Breda, had said the Tambourine Bar was always heaving full of hunky Northsiders. She looked around and all she could see were the weeds of the Northside. The hunks were not out that night. The white wine was warm and bland. A few poor excuses for manhood approached her, but she gave them the glare that sent them into fast retreat. That was it. She had tried the Northside and found it wanting. Mr John Madison it would be.

She got a tuk-tuk back to Connolly. Sweet helpful little grey-haired man, the driver. Was there anything he could get her? He could get anything. Why she said it, she could never remember. But say it she did.

'You want coca cola? You shall have coca cola.'

Little grey-haired man came to a stop. Spoke to his mobile. Spun down to Henry Street. Stopped by a little lady with a girl in a push chair.

The little lady looked ever so sweet.

Fifty euro per gramme.

Lavinia took two. She wondered if she had been overcharged. Lavinia wouldn't be taking it. She knew it zapped the brain cells, restricted blood supply to the heart, and zonks of other unpleasant things, but sometimes it is handy to have these things for others. You never knew when these things would be useful.

She caught the Dart home and cuddled up on the sofa with a take-away curry watching films from a porn website. She had never realised that there were so many sites. One she kept watching over and over. It was that man with the moustache. He just kept going and going. What a hunk! And he was so like Mr John Madison.

Mumsy rang. Had Lavinia seen that night's episode of the *Amalfi Way* soap? No. Shame. She should watch it. There were successful women that Lavinia could use as role models. Needed to push yourself in life and go after what you want. You need to go to college and get a good degree. Become a lawyer. Become a doctor. Become anything except a teacher or a Catholic priest.

'I couldn't become a Catholic priest, Mumsy. I'm a girl.'

'I knew there was some reason I had a girl.'

Now Lavinia knew that Mumsy was right. She should have gone to college. She would go to Trinity next September. Nice and handy for everything including BT. She would become a solicitor. She didn't fancy becoming a doctor. Doctors deal with nasty things like blood and peoples' piles. Imagine sitting down in Chapter One with a piece of rare meat when you've spent an afternoon looking at deformities in peoples' back passages. Enough to make you a vegetarian.

~

The next day she had an encounter with Mrs Sheila Duffy.

'I know what you're up to Lavinia. It won't work.'

'What's that, Sheila?'

'You know exactly what I mean.'

'I am sure I don't. Please tell me.'

'Just leave poor Mr Madison alone. He is married. His wife, Victoria, is a lovely woman.'

'Oh, Sheila, don't think that I would ever try to come between a man and his wife.'

'Oh. Well, if that really is the case, I apologise. You did spend a long time with him in the photocopying room.'

'He was explaining something to me and I'm a bit of a slow leaner. Let me get you some coffee.'

'Thank you, Lavinia. Sorry if I got that wrong.'

You will be sorry, thought Lavinia.

At lunchtime, Lavinia thought it might be an idea for the two of them to lunch together. Get to know each other. Queen's Head.

Lavinia insisted on getting the drinks while Sheila grabbed a seat by the window. They both had the chowder.

'See you back at the office, Sheila. I'm just popping into Supervalu for a lottery ticket.'

Into Supervalu she went. 'Two lines for tonight's draw and a naggin. Paddy Powers please.'

Later that afternoon, poor Sheila acted very strangely. She giggled a lot and kept going into Mr Madison's office on the pretence of looking for files. She swayed in her seat as she sang old pop songs. Then she felt very sick. She staggered a bit. Mr Madison thought she ought to go home. Mr Madison saw her over to the Dart. She lived just up in Dun Laoghaire.

When he came back, he noted there was a strong smell of whiskey coming from Sheila's desk. In contrast, when Lavinia came into his office to help him, there was this heavenly scent. With Sheila absent Lavinia stepped into her shoes and worked that afternoon with John Madison on the prospectus for Dalkey Donkeys plc, the new company he was setting up for a client.

'I hope you don't mind me asking, Lavinia, but did Sheila have much to drink this lunchtime?'

'I'd rather not say, Mr Madison. I just had an orange. She might have been thirsty. It was rather hot.'

Lavinia did not mention of course that she had felt sorry for sad Sheila and added a little 'coca cola' pick-up powder to her drink. Perhaps she had been a tad too generous with the amount.

It was then that John Madison promoted Lavinia to his personal assistant. He didn't feel he could rely on Sheila anymore if she had a drink problem.

~

Later that evening Lavinia was just about to settle in for a night with that hunky man with the moustache. These porn films were so additive. There was little storyline, but the prowess was magnificent. He was such a fine piece of beef and he went on and on. Such endurance must be such a delight to the lucky girl on the receiving end.

Then the doorbell. What a hunk. All Detective Sergeant Kevin Fingleton needed was a moustache. Never mind the mousy little woman beside him. The mousy woman was a Detective Inspector. Honestly, dear Garda Commissioner, these ranks are the wrong way around. Even Lavinia could see that by just looking at them.

Oh no. Poor Liam O'Dell's body had been recovered from Killiney beach earlier today.

'That's awful. Poor Liam. He was in such a state when I last saw him. We had breakfast together in the Corner Note two mornings ago. He asked to meet. He kept saying it was all too much for him, but he wouldn't say what it was. I walked with him as far as Coliemore Harbour but then I had to get to work. He was going onto Dillon's Park. Poor Liam. I tried so hard to calm him down. I failed.' The tears flowed.

'You wouldn't know if he had a mobile phone with him when you had breakfast together? We have been trying to find it.'

'He said he had lost everything. I didn't know what he meant by that. So sad.' The tears morphed into loud weeping mode. Sergeant Kevin was moved. Inspector Mousy was unmoved.

'You don't know where he spent the night before. Was it with you?' asked Mousy.

'Certainly not. I'm a respectable girl.'

~

Next morning, Lavinia heard part of a telephone call between John Madison and his wife, Victoria. She would be away for a few days. He said he would be spending the evenings with his model engines.

'I would just love to see some of these engines. They

41

must be just such fun puffing away.'

'If you're free, I'll run you round after work and show you my workshop.'

She slipped home at lunchtime and slipped into her red minidress.

In the workshop, he was all over the place. The clumsiness of shyness. He dropped one of the engines. They stooped down together. She reached and touched his hand. They both took hold of the engine at the same time. There was a little tug of war over the engine, followed by giggles. As they stood up, they both hit their heads on the table. She lost her balance. He pulled her up and she pushed herself into his arms. They kissed.

They didn't stop kissing. Love in the workshop was a vertical affair. This man had all the vigour and stamina Lavinia yearned for. He ran her home and stayed the night. Act two was horizontal and sustained.

The next few days were heaven. Lavinia's lust was satisfied daily. John Madison was in love.

There were the inevitable problems when his wife, Victoria, returned home. John tried to end the affair with Lavinia.

It is over. It was just a one-nighter.

'Whatever you say, John. I'll do whatever you want and, remember, if you change your mind ...'

~

John was restless in the office. He found it hard to concentrate. Every time he saw Lavinia she seemed to do that sweet little smile that turned his legs to jelly. His relationship with his wife plunged. He found it hard when she was intimate with him. He started to find her proximity repulsive. He started to resent her. Resentment ate into him and turned to hatred.

All the time he kept returning to those words: 'Remember, if you change your mind ...'

All the time at work, he kept looking at Lavinia's figure and yearning for it. He couldn't concentrate. Either Victoria or Lavinia had to go, and it certainly wouldn't be Lavinia.

Over breakfast one morning as he sliced open his boiled egg, he visualised cutting Victoria's throat. She deserved it. She was in the way. Enraged, he went over to the cutlery draw and quietly took out a boning knife. He would go behind her while she was sitting. Hold her by her hair and cut her throat. He went to do it but couldn't muster the nerve.

She turned.

'What on earth are you doing with that knife, John?'

'Oh, nothing. I just needed a sharp blade in the workshop.'

'Put it back. I'm not having my knives blunted by you playing with your toys.'

'I hate it when you call my engines "toys".'

He went to the dressing room, took out one of his scarves and knotted it. He would strangle her. Again, he went up behind her, but couldn't summon up the nerve to do it.

Victoria found the scarf and put it away. She wondered why he had it out. He had been acting very oddly of late. It must be something at work. She decided to find out. First thing next day, she rang his personal assistant, Lavinia.

~

Lavinia and Victoria lunched at The Corkscrew. The conversation never got to John. Lavinia was so entertaining. She made Victoria laugh and giggle. She sounded like a complete scatterhead at first, but then she showed such a good appreciation of music and the arts. Victoria remembered that Lavinia's mother was an opera fan and her father owned a Southside art gallery. What a contrast to John who only wanted to watch football and fiddle around with his toy engines.

The next evening, Lavinia met Victoria at the Dart Station and they went up to the Gate to see *The Snapper*. Pre-theatre dinner at Chapter One. Post-theatre drinks at the Gresham.

At Connelly, just as the train came in, Victoria stumbled. Lavinia caught her and stopped her falling onto the track. Victoria was so appreciative.

Lavinia felt good, but she wondered if she should have stood back and let the Dart train do Mr John Madison's work. She looked at Victoria. No, she had done the right thing. It would have been a shame to spoil that lovely Kooples dress. Perhaps if she had been in tracky bottoms and a Drap top, she could have waved her good-bye, but not when she was wearing Kooples.

Besides, *The Snapper* had been hilarious. They were still laughing on the Dart home.

Did Lavinia fancy a day's shopping with Victoria? Take a sickie. She did. They met at the Dun Laoghaire Dart. Breakfast at the Restaurant. Spent the morning in BT.

The sales assistant thought they were sisters. *We could be*, thought Lavinia. Standing in the fitting room in their undies they looked at each other. Same height. Same dress size. Same bra size. Same eye colour and complexion. The only differences were the hair style and five years in age.

'You are so beautiful, Lavinia.'

'I was just thinking the same about you.'

'And where on earth did you get that bra and that brief? It is *so* you. I must get them too.'

44

They both had a stack of shopping but decided now that they wanted a signature piece to mark their new-found sisterhood—so they would be togged out in the same outfit. Out came the dresses one by one. Stella McCartney, The Kooples, Dolce & Gabbana, Zimmermann, Alexander McQueen, Max Mara. Exhausted sales assistants heaved with relief when the final choice was down to two. Which one of the two? The Valentino lipstick print or the Gabriela Hearst black Larrington off-the-shoulder dress? No discussion. They each took both dresses. They decided to wear the Larrington dresses home, so the poor sales assistants disappeared to bring up a selection of tonal flats.

They got back to Sorrento Drive early afternoon and spent a couple of hours going through Lavinia's wardrobe. Each trying on and parading around in the dresses and tops. Victoria had to borrow that Stella McCartney for lunch the next day with her business associate. It was so her. When Lavinia modelled the little minidress, Victoria went wild.

'And that only cost so much? No wonder it sends them wild. You have such legs.'

And so, for the next few weeks, Lavinia had great fun with her new-found friend. Lunches, theatre, cinema, shopping trips and a spa break at the Adare Manor. Neither mentioned it to John Madison. To Lavinia, it wasn't really his business. To Victoria, her husband was so distant and acting so oddly, she was just relieved to be with someone else.

~

As the weeks passed, John got desperate. He constantly thought of Lavinia. To make matters worse, she kept disappearing at lunchtimes, taking sickies and going to funerals. She must be seeing another man. Enough was enough.

One lunchtime, John took decisive action. He marched Lavinia out to his car and drove round to her little house. They emerged an hour and a half later. Him looking guilty. She with a quiet smile. That evening, long after everyone else had left the office John proposed to Lavinia.

'There is just one little detail John. You already have a wife.'

'I'll divorce her.'

'Are you sure this is what you want? I want it. I love you, but you must be sure, John, it is what you want. All I want to do is make you happy.'

The thought of the hunk on tap appealed, but she would be sorry to lose Victoria as a friend. Let's face it, good girl friends aren't easy to find.

Lavinia agreed to wait until he told Victoria before telling the world. Meanwhile, lunchtimes and the occasional evening in Sorrento Drive kept that quiet smile on Lavinia's face.

~

After a month Lavinia asked the question.

'Are we really engaged? Will you ever tell Victoria?'

'There are problems with just telling her and getting a divorce. She has lots of friends in Dalkey. I would get no business. She would ruin me.'

'Well, we could move. You must have plenty of money to start again somewhere new.'

'The house is Victoria's. She has all the money and she made me sign a pre-nup. I get nothing if I divorce her. She will call in the money I borrowed from her to set up the practice. I will be bankrupted. It could take a year to get a divorce. It would better to kill her. I'd inherit everything. We could marry without impediment.'

'Kill her? You must be joking. Why not divorce her and live with me in Sorrento Drive. It's small, but it's big enough for two.'

'That's the point Lavinia. It isn't big enough. Where would I keep my steam engines? I need to keep the house and the workshop.'

'Oh. My. God. You are going to kill your wife, so you have somewhere to keep your steam engines! That is so crazy. It would be frightening if you weren't joking. You are joking, aren't you?'

'Of course, I'm joking, but think about it. It's a nice clean way to end the marriage. No acrimony. Financially beneficial. We get a house and investments worth upwards of five million. Could be lots of fun doing it and we could marry immediately. Death is a far cleaner way to end a marriage than divorce.'

Lavinia had some serious thinking to do. It would be good to have the wedding ring on her finger, but she also valued her friendship with Victoria. And could John be trusted? He had been unfaithful to Victoria. He might be unfaithful to Lavinia. Perhaps a good friend was more valuable than a husband who could not be trusted.

~

Next day, as John got dressed after their lunchtime entanglement in Sorrento Drive, he asked: 'Well, Lavinia, have you thought anymore about my little suggestion? Death is a lot cleaner way to end a marriage than divorce. We could do it together. Then you'd be my alibi, and I'd be yours.'

'There are times, John, when I don't know if you are serious and just joking. Which is it?'

'You choose and let me know.'

Lavinia was unsure as to what to do. She decided to

keep her own counsel. Becoming Mrs John Madison without the unpleasantness of a divorce and keeping the matrimonial home and fortune had its attractions. However, money was not a great issue to Lavinia. Daddy had deep pockets. Her main concern was that if Victoria was for the chop now, would Lavinia also be for the chop a few years down the line. Perhaps she should give the Northside another chance?

~

The following morning Lavinia had a call from Victoria. Could she come up to the house about 12.30?

There were two places laid on the kitchen table. Two plates of feta cheese and black olive salad. A sourdough loaf.

'I thought I would do lunch, Lavinia. You are such a good friend to me. I have a big favour to ask of you. Sit down.'

Lavinia sat down. She sensed something was wrong.

'I believe John may be having an affair and I want you to help me find out who it is.'

'Why do you think that?'

'I had supper with two of my friends from our reading group. They had both seen John parking up in Sorrento Drive and visiting a young lady. Apparently, he does it most days. Then it occurred to me. Lavinia lives in Sorrento Drive. Lavinia will be able to find out who it is.'

'It's me.'

'I know what you mean, Lavinia, when you say it's not you. You would feel uncomfortable trying to expose someone, but I need your help. Please help me.'

'No, Victoria. I didn't say it's not me. I said it *was* me. It's me he visits in Sorrento Drive. We spend most lunchtimes together.'

'Well, what a relief! That explains everything. You see, Lavinia, I know your little secret. Your mother told me. I know you are studying law and are going up to Trinity next September. Quite right too. You've a fine mind and you should use it. And ten out of ten to John for helping you with your studies. I'm so pleased for you and so proud of him. I am so relieved that it is all so innocent. Your mother always tells me how lucky I am having John as my husband. She's right. He might be a bit dull at times, but he is really nice.'

'Oh, Victoria, I feel so bad.'

'Don't be silly Lavinia. You should be proud of yourself, studying again.'

'No, you don't understand. My lunchtimes with John are not innocent. We are having an affair.'

'No, no. I'm not hearing this. This is not happening. You can't be having an affair with my husband. You are my friend. My best friend. You, Lavinia, are the only one I trust. You wouldn't do that. John might, but you wouldn't. You couldn't. You wouldn't betray me. Tell me it is not true.'

'It is true. I'm so sorry but I did betray you.'

'I would have given you anything you asked for. How do you repay me? You screwed my husband. How often did you do it? How long has it been going on?'

Victoria stood there, silent. There were tears furrowing her make-up. Her mascara ran. Her shoulders hunched, her back partly bent. She wanted to scream. She wanted to wail.

Lavinia, moved to compassion, went to hug her, but Victoria backed off and strode across to the draining board. Out from the kitchen drawer came the boning knife.

Victoria advanced on Lavinia. Lavinia managed to grab Victoria's wrist and keep the knife away, but then disaster struck. The heel of Lavinia's left shoe broke. Lavinia lost her balance and she was on the floor stunned, lying face upwards. Victoria knelt down on top of her. The knife was in Victoria's hand.

'Say something, you Judas.' Victoria wept. 'I expected *him* to be unfaithful, but not you. Why you? We were such special friends.'

'I'm so sorry, Victoria. What can I say? We are still special friends.'

'My own sweet dearest friend, you betrayed me. You fucked my husband. You fucked him again and again.'

Lavinia didn't know what to say. She tried to wriggle to free herself. It was impossible. She was Victoria's prisoner. Victoria's knees pinned Lavinia's arms.

'Say your prayers, you Judas. You will die.'

'But, Victoria, you can't.'

'Oh yes, I can, Lavinia, dear. I'm going to kill you. I will bury you in the garden. I will plant a little cherry tree over you. Each year, when it's in flower I'll think of you. I'll call it Lavinia's tree. Now bye-bye my friend, my sweet, sweet friend. How I loved, loved you to the end.'

Victoria raised her hand to strike the fatal blow, but her hand was caught by John, who had quietly tiptoed into the kitchen unseen by the two women.

A fierce struggle followed. John, Victoria and Lavinia were wrestling with each other, each trying to get control of the knife.

Eventually, Lavinia won the contest. There she was, knife in hand, facing Victoria.

John just stood there shouting, 'Kill her, Lavinia, kill her!

Victoria acknowledged defeat. She put her hands up and turned her face away, eyes closed, waiting for the blow.

Lavinia looked at Victoria's white lace dress and imagined it covered in blood. She looked at Victoria. She imagined, in horror, that beautiful body limp and dead. She could spoil neither the dress nor the person. She threw the knife to one side and hugged Victoria.

'Forgive me.'

They cried together but not for long.

John had retrieved the knife and was rushing at Victoria. Lavinia stepped across. Victoria gasped. It appeared as if the knife would go into Lavinia, but, then, all of a sudden, John was thrown to the floor. Lavinia was delighted. She had executed a perfect Tanto Dori defence move. Mr Matsumoto would be so pleased.

Victoria hugged Lavinia and then addressed John. 'Get out of this house and never return. I'll have your things sent on.'

'No,' Lavinia said, 'we can't let John go like this. He is all shaken up. Look how white he is. He's in shock. He could have an accident driving like that. I'll make him a sweet cup of tea first.

They all had tea, in silence. John thought his tea tasted odd. He didn't say anything.

He turned just once on the way out. Victoria shouted, 'Go!'

Afterwards, Victoria confided to Lavinia that she was frightened John might come back, knife in hand.

Lavinia smiled. 'Don't worry, dearest. He won't do that.'

~

A year later, as she sliced open her boiled egg one morning, Lavinia looked across the kitchen table at Victoria and smiled again.

It had been a traumatic year for Victoria. First, losing her husband, John, in that tragic single vehicle accident on Vico Road. The shame of it, with him being high on coke.

She knew John had done coke as a lad but had no idea he was still doing it. Then her mother died. Then she had found romance again with her best friend.

In the drawing room was a lovely framed photo of the couple on their wedding day in those identical dresses.

For Lavinia it had also been a dramatic year. A year of new beginnings. She was now an undergraduate at Trinity and a married woman. She looked lovingly at her partner. It had been a hard year for her but at least Victoria hadn't had to go through a painful divorce. As someone once said, 'Death is a lot cleaner way to end a marriage than divorce.'

One thing Victoria never understood. Occasionally, of an evening, Lavinia would smile and raise her glass. If asked, she would just say, 'I am toasting a little grey haired tuk-tuk man I once met.'

He who is not contented with what he has would not be contented with what he would like to have.

~ **Socrates**

Rhythm of the Sea

Adrian Taheny

Twelve, thirteen, fourteen, fifteen. Turn ... One, two, three ...

John Kinkade was unaware that he was counting every stroke or that he had his eyes fixed on the line of black tiles that stretched end to end on the floor of his pool. He was obsessed with swimming in a straight line. Having to take a breath every few strokes annoyed him at first as it threw him off centre, and he had to adjust his position each time. These added up and interrupted his train of thought during his daily swim of one hour. He used this time to consider many things. He had a great deal to think about.

~

Eight, nine, ten, eleven ...

The cops came with the bad news when he was only eight years old. He held onto his mother's hand in the doorway of their small house.

'I'm afraid your husband is dead, Mrs Kinkade. Witnesses say he was drunk and shouting abuse before he threw himself in front of the train.'

His father's only legacy: bad debts and bad memories.

'You gotta make something of yourself, John. You gotta do good in life.'

'I will, Momma. I promise.'

He helped out. After school, he did odd jobs and gave her any money he earned. The letter from Cornell confirming his place in the College of Veterinary Medicine arrived the day after she died. This was his ticket to a better future. He was going to do good in life.

~

Twelve, thirteen, fourteen, fifteen. Turn ... One, two, three ...

Felix Madison was from Avery Island, Louisiana, where his father was the local vet. It was known as the home of Tabasco. He was nicknamed 'Hot Sauce' on campus, but Felix didn't pay much heed to what people called him. It never bothered him. He roomed with John Kinkade in college and they became close friends.

'You're like a second brother to me,' Felix said. I never got to know my twin. He died when we were born. I got out first. He didn't make it.'

'Only the strongest shall survive, my brother,' was John Kinkade's reply.

Evenings were often spent in their room sharing stories and making plans for the future. Felix would talk about all the people who travelled from far and wide to visit his father, the local vet, for the cure. Whether it was hypertension or depression, inflammation or infection, hot flushes or cold, his father could cure it. With a pinch of salt.

'We came from the sea and we need the salt,' his father would say.

Felix explained that long before Tabasco, Avery Island was known for its rich deposits of salt. Native Americans boiled the briny spring water to extract salt, then traded it with other tribes as far away as central Texas, Arkansas and Ohio. The healing and restorative properties it contained had been recognised as far back as records go.

His father never gave his secrets away. Not to his patients. They wouldn't believe that a simple pinch of salt could make such a difference. So, once he established the problem and the extent of it, he would give them a mixture to take over a specified period. And his success rate was phenomenal.

'"You are the salt of the earth", he would say to me, "and you will be the fourth generation Madison in this practice."'

'You don't sound too enthusiastic?'

'I want my life to be different. Better.'

'We'll start a business, Felix.'

'We'll cure the world, John.'

'We'll make a fortune, Felix.'

~

Eight, nine, ten, eleven …

Then Bonnie came along. Felix met her back in '79 at a music festival in her hometown of Los Angeles. He was there to see Cheech & Chong. She went to hear a new Irish punk band called The Boomtown Rats. But he quickly discovered they had something in common. She was doing pharmacy at Cornell. They spent a crazy weekend together and by the time they got back to college, they were nuts about each other.

'John, this is Bonnie O'Brien. Her folks own a chain of drugstores in California called Jack & Jill.'

Two friends became three and they delighted in each other's company. Felix and Bonnie grew closer with each semester. And John would avail of every opportunity to chat with her about his plans for the future. About his theories on old remedies and cures and how they might be adapted for a new business.

'Felix, tell Bonnie about your father's cure. Tell her about the pinch of salt.'

One day, Bonnie figured it out.

'Every body needs a specific mix of sodium and potassium to function normally. Too much or too little of one or the other and there's a problem. Your Dad was sorting out the sodium side. With salt!'

~

Felix was impressed, but he had no time to follow up on her conclusion. He was already struggling to make his grades. John Kinkade had other ideas. Bigger ideas. He would spend days upon end in the library studying medical journals and traditional remedies. Then long conversations would follow with Bonnie, testing out his theories on her. Felix began to find their intensity too much for him and more often than not, he left them at it. Graduating was important for him. His father's health was deteriorating, and the practice needed a successor if it was to survive. There was little he could do as Bonnie and John spent more and more time together.

'We will keep in touch,' Bonnie said as she kissed him goodbye after the graduation.

'Yes, hopefully,' he replied as he watched her jump into John Kinkade's car.

An hour later, Felix had started his own journey back to Avery Island. It would take him a couple of days to get there. The image of Bonnie with John Kinkade plagued him, and his sense of betrayal grew deeper with every mile. He felt angry and alone.

~

Twelve, thirteen, fourteen, fifteen. Turn … One, two, three …

John Kinkade married Bonnie O'Brien soon after they finished college. Not everyone thought it was a good idea. They didn't have a red cent between them, but she believed in him and that was all that mattered. They did have hopes and dreams for the future and they had each other. She insisted on sending Felix an invitation. She never heard from him and he did not turn up on the day.

As a wedding gift, her father, Jack O'Brien, offered John a partnership in a small drug manufacturing operation he had in California. He saw his opportunity and jumped at the chance. It was clear from the start that the business was small ticket and going nowhere. They made and sold very basic products that were out of patent elsewhere and, in most cases, had been replaced with a newer product from one or other of the major pharmaceutical companies. It needed new life. A new product with their own patent. John Kinkade already had the answer. And he had a pharmacist by his side that would help him deliver.

'Sodium and potassium. We need to develop a series of tests and a range of drugs to re-balance the system,' he declared.

It took ten years of hard work and determination to raise the money, develop the test protocols and a new suite of drugs. He encountered objections from every corner of the industry and intense scrutiny and demands from the regulator. He was determined to succeed. To become a major player. Nothing and nobody was going to stop him.

Finally, the FDA granted approval and Xpulex hit the market. Within months it was receiving rave reviews across the medical journals and, eventually, the general media. It became the prescription drug for primary care physicians. The key ingredients in the mix remained a closely guarded secret, known only to the small group of scientists working at Xpulex headquarters. This same group continued to develop new versions of the drug to effectively treat muscle inflammation, chronic fatigue, anxiety and heart disorders.

~

For thirty-five years Bonnie was his soulmate, his lover and his business partner. She took care of the kids, while he drove their business, Xpulex, to annual revenues of fifteen billion. Their personal net worth was put at five billion in the Forbes rich list the year Bonnie got sick.

~

Eight, nine, ten, eleven …

Their endowment to the Smithsonian was named 'The Kinkade' and it would support future generations of professionals and innovators in history, science, art and culture, attached to the institute. Normally shy of any publicity, they were advised to go public on this occasion because of the scale of their gift. John and Bonnie signed the necessary documents in the morning, posed for photos, enjoyed lunch with the Board of Regents and then flew back in their private jet. Bonnie complained of a pain in her back as they were driven home. A couple of weeks later, her closest friend, Maggie, suggested that her colour was off and that she should see someone about it.

'It's stage three,' the consultant confirmed. 'Treatment is not an option. Symptom relief is key from now on.'

John Kinkade had flown his wife to the Mayo Clinic in Minnesota to get the best medical help available and this was not what he wanted to hear. He would look for a second opinion. He would call on the leading experts from around the world. He knew powerful people in the industry. They would have to help him save Bonnie.

Two days after they got home, Bonnie was rushed to hospital with breathing problems and a pain in her chest. After extensive tests, it was diagnosed as a blood clot in a large vein in her leg. A piece had broken off and travelled into her lungs.

'It's deep-vein thrombosis and, unfortunately, she has also developed a pulmonary embolism,' the consultant explained. 'I'm afraid it is only a matter of time.'

~

Twelve, thirteen, fourteen, fifteen. Turn … One, two, three …

Felix Madison arrived at Xpulex headquarters and insisted on speaking with John Kinkade.

'Mr Kinkade is not available right now,' the receptionist told him.

'Tell Mr Kinkade that I'm not leaving until we talk.'

What could he want? We haven't been in touch since college days. Was it about Bonnie? Did he know she was ill? Or about something else? That we didn't keep in touch with him over the years?

'I'll pick him up at reception on my way out,' John Kinkade told his secretary.

The two men walked in the park across from Xpulex HQ. Felix looked anxious and unwell.

'What ya been up to since college days, Felix?'

Very little as it turned out. After college Felix went back to Avery Island to help out with the practice. His dad was poorly at the time, and he got stuck there. Next thing he knows, both parents are dead, and he's left with a failing veterinary business. That went too.

'We live in hurricane country down in Louisiana. Can't get insurance. Place got hit. I borrowed some money from the bank to get back in business. Two years later and we get hit again.'

The last ten years were a struggle. Then one day he sees his old friend John Kinkade and his wife Bonnie on the front of Forbes Magazine.

'Bonnie's not well. I suppose you heard.'

'Yea, I heard something. And I am sorry. But that's not why I'm here. We had a deal.'

'A deal. What deal?'

'We were going to set up a business, cure the world, remember.'

'I don't get it Felix.'

'We were going to make a fortune, you said.'

'Ok, now I get it. In college. That nonsense.'

'You stole my idea and you stole my girl.'

'Bonnie? You think I stole her?'

'With all your fancy talk about sodium and potassium and your big plans, you turned her away from me.'

'You lost interest. You started doing your own thing.'

'I could never keep up with you. I needed to study. To graduate. For the practice on Avery Island.'

'What do you want?'

'I want my share. That's the least I deserve.'

'You're mad Felix. I've built up this business with Bonnie and I'm dammed if I'm handing one cent of it over to you.'

'I told you about my father. About his cures. I told you everything. You owe me.'

'Felix, you need help. And not from me. You should see someone.'

~

Eight, nine, ten, eleven …

'I had a visitor today. At the office.'

Bonnie tried to smile and look interested, but she was numb from the pain relief drugs that were pouring into her body through a drip.

'It was Felix. Felix Madison. You remember Hot Sauce?'

Her face softened at the mention of his name. Sweet memories of music festivals and college days flooded her brain cells. He could see the change in her. Felix had meant a great deal to Bonnie. John Kinkade tried to convince himself that she was better off with him. Felix was going nowhere. And look at all they had achieved together over the years.

'He's not in good shape.'

The softness disappeared from her face and a tear came to her eye.

'He's looking for help. I told him he needed to go and see someone else.'

Bonnie drew on all the strength she had left inside her and slowly shook her head.

~

Twelve, thirteen, fourteen, fifteen. Turn ... One, two, three ...

In a private room at the Bohemian Club on 624 Taylor Street, San Francisco, four men sat down to lunch. Two had flown in from New York. The third from Boston. Between them, they controlled close to fifty per cent of oncology revenues, annually. The fourth man was John Kinkade. All were on first name terms and had much in common. After a light lunch and some shared wisdom on worldly matters, the conversation turned to address the main reason behind their meeting: Bonnie's illness. John Kinkade had called them together in the hope that they would provide him with a cure for his wife's cancer. Access to a new drug. In development. In confidence.

The three men listened to his pleas for help. They glanced about the table but did not respond. Each of them held a key to discoveries that could change the world. But turning that key would change their worlds too. Make so much of what they sold, redundant. The patents on some of their drugs had years to run. John Kinkade rose from his seat and pleaded with them once more.

'You've got to help me'

'It doesn't exist,' said one.

'Jesus Christ, she's dying.'

'You know the protocol, John. A cure does not exist for cancer,' said another.

'It's my wife, for God's sake.'

'We treat cancer, John. We don't cure it,' said the third.

'Who the fuck do you three think you are? You actually believe you can put a price on life and a time on death. It's wrong. All of it!'

~

Eight, nine, ten, eleven ...

After Bonnie's funeral, he was alone. He had promised her he would find a way. He had promised their kids that he would save her. He had failed them all. He walked aimlessly through the house they had planned and built together for something that was no longer there. Upstairs, he lay on the bed where they had shared their hopes, their dreams and each other. He grabbed her pillow and pulled it tightly into his face to smell her scent. It wasn't there.

Without Bonnie by his side, Xpulex was worthless. It had delivered so much for them in life, but in the face of death, it failed them. He retired from his role as Executive Chairman soon after she died. The Board looked after it now. None of his own children were involved. Bonnie always wanted them to find their own way in life and they did.

He thought a great deal about Felix Madison too. Looking back on their days in college. Their plans and dreams to cure the world. To make a fortune. Together. And Felix was right about Bonnie. She was his girl.

~

Twelve, thirteen, fourteen, fifteen. Turn ... One, two, three ...

One week later, John Kinkade sat in front of his TV and, at precisely 10 a.m., he flicked it on, just in time to hear Betty Liu of Bloomberg introduce her exclusive interview with him, recorded the previous day.

'Why now?' Betty asked him.

'Because, hopefully, it's not too late.'

'Too late for what?'

'To change. To take back control.'

'From who? Control of what?'

'From a small group of individuals who make billions every year, playing God with our lives.'

'What are you proposing to do about it?'

'With immediate effect, I am transferring control of all

the resources and reserves at Xpulex to the World Health Organisation.'

'And …?'

'I will cooperate fully with any investigations that are initiated into practices within the industry.'

Down in Louisiana, the phone rang in Felix Madison's home. It was his bank manager. He needed to speak urgently with Felix in his office. Foreclosure on the house and lands on Avery Island seemed inevitable. A large loan outstanding and no prospect of paying it back.

'Felix ain't here. He's gone away for a few days. This is his wife, Jan.'

'Hold on Mrs Madison. I'll let you talk with your attorney, Jim McIlhenny. He's here with me now. *He* will explain everything.'

'Betty, we have some very good news. A wealthy benefactor has arranged a transfer of $10 million into your husband's account at the bank. You and your family don't have anything to worry about, ever again.'

~

Eight, nine, ten, eleven …

The pool came with the house. Part of the trappings of success. He couldn't remember when he started to swim every day or when he first noticed the black line of tiles on the floor. And now he was counting every stroke he took. He felt constrained. Locked into a routine that was not his own. It felt unnatural. He heard his dog barking in the distance. Bonnie had insisted on taking him home from the Puppy Rescue. She called him Salty. The barking grew louder. He was swimming into the setting sun and could just about make out the shape of a man pointing something at the dog by the pool. Then the awful sound of a gunshot. Piercing. Echoing into the distance. The barking stopped.

John Kinkade didn't make it to the end of the pool. He stopped and treaded water in the deep end, wiping his eyes to try and see out what had just happened. The rays from the sun blurred his vision and his head was spinning from the loud bang. He could just make out the figure of a man turning towards him. He had what looked like a gun in his hand. He pointed it in the air and fired again. That piercing sound rang out once more. The echo seemed to go on and on. The dog lay motionless on the poolside.

'Stay exactly where you are, John Kinkade.'

It was the voice of Felix Madison.

'You told me to see someone. I did. He sold me this Magnum 44!'

A third shot into the air. The noise was deafening. It reverberated inside John Kinkade's head. Felix looked down at the dog.

'Ugly hound. Bull Mastiff. I never cared much for animals.'

'What do you want Felix?'

'Already told you what I wanted.' He said waving the gun in the air.

John Kinkade was beginning to struggle to stay up in the three meters of water. He moved his body in an effort to get closer to the side of the pool. A fourth shot rang out. He head was spinning from the noise.

'Stay right where you are or the next one is for you.'

'I've tried to put things right. I made a call.'

'It's too late for that now. You were meant to be like kin to me. You were going to be my brother. Remember?'

He remembered Felix telling him about his twin who didn't make it. How he got out first. He remembered calling him brother back in Cornell.

'You said only the fittest survive. Remember? You were right. And now it's your time to go.'

John Kinkade was kicking hard to keep his head above the water. He had counted four shots. At least one bullet left. Maybe two.

'You stole my ideas ... you stole my girl ... you stole my life. Now it's payback time.'

'Please, Felix.' John Kinkade was gulping water into his lungs. He went under.

'Help me, Felix!' For a second time, he went under.

He heard the Magnum fire again as he sank beneath the water for the third time.

~

'Your husband is dead Mrs Kinkade.'

'You gotta make something of yourself, John. You gotta do good in life.'

'I will Momma. I promise.'

'Only the strongest shall survive, my brother. You are the salt of the earth. We'll cure the world. We'll make a fortune.'

'Who the fuck do you three think you are?'

'You remember Hot Sauce?'

'Only the fittest shall survive. Only the fittest ...

~

'We didn't think you were going to make it Mr Kinkade.'

'Where am I? What happened?'

I'm Dr Banks and this is Sheriff Flynn. You're in the County Hospital in ICU.'

'We thought you were a goner. Got ya out just in time. Parameds did a great job.'

'Felix. What happened Felix?'

'The other guy. We had reports of gunshots. By the time we got to your place you were at the bottom of the pool and the other guy, Felix, he'd blown his head to bits with a Magnum 44. Looks like he shot the dog too.'

'Sheriff, we need to let Mr Kinkade rest for now. He has a lot to think about.'

'One last thing,' the Sherriff said. 'What were you saying about only the fittest surviving, Mr Kinkade? You were shouting it in your sleep. Just before you came round.'

'I don't remember'.

He didn't want to remember. He had lost everyone and everything he ever cared for. It wasn't about survival anymore. It had become a struggle to exist.

~

When John Kinkade was discharged a week later, he drove hard until he reached the west coast. He stood on the shoreline listening to the pounding noise of the waves breaking before him then gently rolling in and caressing his bare feet. His heart soared inside.

Now he swims in an ocean without boundaries. There is no painted line to follow. No counting strokes.

The sea imposes its own rhythm and there is no looking back.

As iron is eaten by rust, so are the envious consumed by envy.

~Antisthenes

The Snake that Ate its Own Heart

Alix Moore

Saturday, 13 January 2018

North York Moors, 4.50 a.m.

The road snakes its way across the moors like a silver ribbon carelessly tossed onto the bleak landscape, the snow erasing familiar landmarks as it settles. My heart beats faster than the rapid staccato rhythm of the windscreen wipers, and I struggle not to gag at the sour stench of Shane, his comatose body folded into the passenger seat next to me. I touch his hand, fever-hot skin under my fingertips, and think it the most precious gift in the world at this moment, knowing that it may be the last time.

A burst of static erupts from the loudspeaker on the dashboard. 'Are you there, Kate?'

'Yes.' My voice is thick with unshed tears.

'We lost you there for a bit. The blizzard is playing havoc with our satellite system. How is your husband?'

I glance to my left. His eyes are shut, and his breathing is rapid and shallow. 'I think he's unconscious.'

'When did he last speak to you?'

'About half an hour ago … just after I got him into the car.' His words still echo in my skull, 'Help me, Kate, I think I'm dying.'

'Keep driving, Kate. The ambulance is only a couple of miles away. They've just passed Thoresby Mount.'

I mentally review the situation in preparation for briefing the paramedics. Yesterday afternoon Shane drank about three ounces of antifreeze washed down with alcohol. I'd woken around three this morning and found him collapsed on the landing. When it became obvious how ill he was, I'd decided to try and get him to hospital myself rather than waiting for the ambulance. Shane's condition has deteriorated significantly since we set off and I am terrified that he has now entered the second phase where his kidneys will start to fail, and he will suffer brain damage. Ice-cold fingers of panic claw into my scalp and rake down my back as I face the fact my husband may die, and I start to pray to a god I don't believe in: 'Please God, help Shane. Don't let him die.'

My hands start to cramp from holding the steering wheel in a vice-like grip, and I flex them, relishing the distraction of pain as the blood flows into my bone-white fingertips.

Suddenly, a shimmer of blue lights dance on the horizon. I blink rapidly to clear my vision and sob with relief as I realise that it is the urgent flashing lights of an ambulance heading in our direction.

I stroke Shane's hand and whisper, 'Hold on, love.'

~

Saturday, 21 October 2017—twelve weeks earlier

Micklewell House, North York Moors, 3.37 p.m.

I stand at the front window of my home, a solid, stone-built house which has endured more than two hundred years in the shadow of Micklewell Crag on the North York Moors, and watch my sister's scarlet SUV swing through the gates and bump its way up the pot-holed drive.

I hurry to open the front door and am met by an arctic blast of wind, straight from the North Sea. Mel enters the house like a mini tornado, envelops me in a cold, fragrant hug and shrugs off multiple layers of thermal clothing while she grumbles about 'having to drive through the wilderness, in this dreadful bloody weather, to this godforsaken place in the middle of bloody nowhere—this had better be good, Kate.' I take no notice, knowing that wild horses wouldn't have stopped Mel from coming over to solve the mystery of the 'something urgent I need to speak to you about' I'd mentioned on the phone earlier.

We go into the living room and settle ourselves on the sofas placed on either side of the inglenook fireplace. Mel calls her latest bloke to let him know she's arrived safely, and I feel the usual jealous tug inside as I listen to their easy banter as they make arrangements to meet later. Blokes come easy to Mel.

We're like chalk and cheese, Mel and I. She's four years younger than me and the spitting image of our mother, with her blue eyes, blonde hair and sunny disposition. She gets on with everyone and uses this skill to great effect in her job as Public Relations Director of Brindley's, the brewery which has been in our family for over a hundred years.

I pale by comparison with my unremarkable looks and moody, awkward nature. As a child I believed my parents hadn't tried hard enough when they made me; that they'd saved the best of themselves to put into her. We lost our Mam a few days after my twelfth birthday and, without her to act as referee, envy of my pretty little sister wormed its way in and I started to bully her. Mean, petty stuff at first, like hiding her homework and slashing the tyres on her bike; but it nearly ended in disaster the night I set the curtains in Mel's bedroom on fire while she lay sleeping. My 'heroic' cries of 'fire!' brought Dad running, but, by then, the sparks from the curtain had set an armchair alight and the fire brigade had to be called.

It was obvious that I'd done it, but I stubbornly refused to confess, and the incident blackened not only the house, but my relationship with my father. I still remember his look of bewildered disappointment and what he said to me: 'Envy is self-destructive, it'll eat you alive. Think on it, our Kate.' For weeks after I'd fancied I could feel something snake-like slithering around in my belly and the fear of it had made me very careful to be kinder to Mel, to stifle that undesirable side of my nature.

Mel finishes her call and cuts to the chase. 'What were you up to today? I popped into your office this morning and Betty said you were out 'on a mission'.

'I spent the day in the brew lab working on the new summer stout for EireWay.'

Mel gives me a sharp look. 'Haven't you got enough to do? The brew lab is Philip Harper's baby. Careful you don't tread on his toes with your meddling, he's worth his weight in gold.'

'Don't worry. Phil's cool about it. He's still in charge, I'm just …'

'Interfering?' says Mel sweetly.

'Helping,' I say firmly. 'Cup of tea?'

As I mash the tea, I think back to when I'd joined Brindley's fresh from university, the ink not yet dry on my degree in biochemistry. No gap year for me; I couldn't wait to join the family business and show Dad that I'd changed, prove myself to him. I'd loved those early years in the brew lab, combining science with a touch of magic to develop new flavours and varieties of beers. Dad and I got on much better at work than at home, and he took me under his wing, taught me everything he knew about beer and the brewery business. When he died five years ago, I'd been declared his obvious successor and now spend my days building the business and keeping our shareholders fat and happy.

Mel wanders into the kitchen. 'How's Shane getting on in Ireland?'

I join her at the table. 'He says EireWay like the idea. There isn't anything like it in their stores at the moment, and our bitters and lagers are flying off the shelves apparently. So, they want us to produce a batch of summer stout and they'll test it out in their Galway stores. If it's a success there, they'll consider increasing the contract to cover the whole of Ireland.'

'Good for Shane. He's worked bloody hard on this project.' Mel sips her tea and gives me a sisterly once-over. 'Now then, are you going to tell me what's up? She can spot one of my dog days a mile off.

'… I don't know where to start.'

Something in my voice has Mel as alert as a pointer dog that's found its target, and she says impatiently, 'Good grief, Kate, what's happened?'

I take a deep breath. 'Have you noticed that Shane hasn't been himself for the last six months or so?'

Mel shrugs. 'He's spending so much time in Ireland these days I haven't seen much of him really. But, he's certainly quieter than normal, preoccupied. Have you had a falling out?'

I shake my head miserably. 'I don't know. I'm not sure what's going on.' I fetch an envelope from the dresser and hand it to Mel. 'This arrived a couple of days ago. It was addressed to Shane care of the Galway project office. He was at that sales conference in Germany last week and somebody must have forwarded it here knowing he was coming home for the week. I opened it by accident, but when I saw what it was …'

Mel narrows her eyes. 'What?'

'It's from a firm of solicitors in Galway asking Shane to come into their office to sign a deed of transfer on a property that he has purchased so that it can pass into the sole ownership of a woman called Rose Connolly.'

Mel reads the letter. 'This has to be a mistake, Kate.'

'That's what I thought at first, but I've checked out the firm and they're kosher.'

'Who the hell is Rose Connolly? Has Shane ever mentioned her?

'Never. I have no idea who she is or what her relationship is to Shane.'

Mel glances at the letter again. 'This gives her address, so it shouldn't be difficult to track her down.'

'I've already googled her. She's twenty-eight years old and making a name for herself as a jeweller. Her name's all over the newspapers ... she's quite the celebrity. Apparently, she was commissioned to make some jewellery for a film, the leading lady fell in love with her stuff and started wearing it and'—I snap my fingers—'bingo, everybody's mad for it. She's just opened a shop in Galway.' I open my iPad and pass it over to Mel. 'That's her.'

I sit down next to Mel and we look at the picture in silence. Rose Connolly has the look of a pre-Raphaelite angel with long red hair falling in tangled waves around her perfectly sculpted face, her lips pouted above her cupped hand as if she is blowing a kiss at the photographer.

Mel muses. 'Quite the package, isn't she? But what is she to Shane? And where would he find the money to buy a house? He can't have taken out a mortgage because any application would have to go through our payroll department. I know his salary's good, but you guys don't exactly live like paupers and I can't imagine Shane is a saver!'

I blurt out, 'He's sold £300,000 worth of his Brindley shares.'

'The shares Dad gave him when you got married?'

'Yes.'

Mel looks furious. 'Those shares should have remained in the family. What the hell is he playing at?'

I fix my gaze on the bowl of white hyacinths on the coffee table, their heavy fragrance suddenly almost suffocating in the profound silence of the room. After a minute I say, 'I think he's planning to leave me and set up a new life in Ireland,' and as soon as the words are out of my mouth, I feel something familiar slither its way up through my guts and wrap itself around my heart, filling me with a jealous loathing of Rose Connolly. The lights flicker on and off, a common occurrence in this isolated spot, triggering a shudder of superstitious fear and I start to shake uncontrollably. Mel strokes my hand and murmurs soft words of comfort. I hear our mother in her voice, feel her in the comforting pressure of Mel's cool fingers and hot tears burn their way down my cheeks.

Mel hands me a tissue and says, 'Have you asked Shane what's going on?'

'No. This isn't something that be discussed over the 'phone. I'll talk to him face to face when he gets back tomorrow.' I scrub the tears away impatiently, 'I'm not going to be made a fool of Mel. I'm not letting him go without a fight.'

Mel squeezes my hand. 'Don't go jumping to conclusions. He's a lovely lad and you always seem really happy despite …'

I stiffen, immediately on the defensive. 'Despite what?'

'Despite the fact that sometimes you micromanage your relationship with Shane as if you are running a business. It's as if you just can't relax and enjoy what you have with him.'

I stare at my sister for a minute, everything in me wanting to deny what she has just said. But I can't because Mel knows me inside out and the adult in me knows every word is true. My inner child however chooses to disagree, and I mutter sulkily, 'Thanks for the sermon.'

Mel looks thoughtful. 'You need to be really careful, Kate. I don't think you should say anything to him until you know the facts. There could be a completely plausible explanation for all of this, and if you wade in now it could be the end of your marriage. If Shane bales out of Brindley's, we can probably kiss the EireWay contract goodbye and watch our share prices plummet.'

'So what should I do?'

Mel morphs into control mode. 'Open a bottle of wine, while I ring Joe again and tell him I'm staying here tonight. We have some planning to do. You and I need to get ourselves over to Ireland and find out what's going on with this Rose piece.'

~

Saturday, 13 January 2018

James Cook Hospital, Middlesbrough, 8.29 a.m.

'Mrs Murray?'

I drag my mind from the dark place and raise my head. 'Yes?'

A tall man with tired eyes smiles down at me. 'I'm Ben Thomson. I'll be looking after your husband while he is the Intensive Care Unit.'

'How is he?'

Ben sits down next to me. 'Based on the information you've given us, he's taken a potentially lethal dose ethylene glycol. Because of the time that's elapsed since he ingested it, washing out his gut is not going to be beneficial, so we've started him on a drug called Antizol which will inhibit its effects. Our renal specialist is assessing him now as he may need haemodialysis to remove the ethylene glycol from his blood.'

I get up slowly. 'Can I see him?'

'Of course.' Ben Thomson touches my arm gently. 'And don't be alarmed by all of the tubes and wires; they're there to help him with his breathing and to replace lost fluids.'

I follow him into the IC unit: a vast, white space divided into bed spaces. My head instantly fills with noise: the relentless click and hiss of ventilators breathing life into the almost-dead, the unsynchronised beeping of heart rate monitors, the rip and tear of a Velcro blood pressure arm band being removed. There is an overwhelming smell of disinfectant and decay, and I feel the adrenalin race round my body, urging me to run, to leave this place before it can claim me. But as I see Shane, lying so still and white, I am stopped in my tracks by an overwhelming feeling of love, its familiar cadences and rhythms flowing into me, and I know that I will stay as long as I am allowed to, as long as Shane needs me ... I will stay as long as I can.

I sit by his bed and gently stroke his forehead. He is burning up, and I long to absorb the heat into my body, take his pain away. For what seems like the thousandth time today, I wish that I could turn back the clock, do things differently.

~

Monday, 23 October 2017—twelve weeks earlier

CEO's Office, Brindley's Brewery, Middlesbrough, North Yorkshire, 11.00

Shane throws his arms around me and kisses me gently on the lips. 'God, it's so good to see you, Katy.' I'm as stiff as a dressmaker's dummy in his embrace, and he releases me. 'What's the matter darling?'

I scowl. 'Nothing. I'm OK.'

Shane frowns. 'Well, you don't look or sound OK.'

I force myself to smile, but it's a poor effort, as if my mouth has forgotten which shape it should make. 'Sorry. I'm just tired. It's been pretty full on here.'

We sit on the leather sofa and Shane takes my hand, his thumb tenderly smoothing the skin at the base of my thumb. I immediately wonder whether he does this to Rose and pull my hand away.

He chuckles a little and nudges me. 'So, tell me what's going on, then. Were you missing me?' He obviously thinks I am in one of my moods and is trying to jolly me out of it.

I can almost hear Mel's voice saying, 'For God's sake, Kate, pull yourself out of it or he'll know something's up,' so I laugh—a harsh, brittle imitation of the genuine article—and say, 'I always miss you.'

It's true. I hate it when he's not around. Shane paints my life in bright, vibrant colours, quite unlike the monochrome existence I led before we got together. He's the only person who has ever called me Katy, the name doesn't suit me. But eight years ago, when he breezed into Brindley's, twenty-six years old and brimming over with the abundant charm for which Irish men are famous, it was one of the many things that he got away with.

He was an extraordinarily gifted salesman and Dad really took to him; I can remember him saying, 'Young Shane Murray is one to watch. He reckons he can sell Brindley's beer to the Irish and have them believing that it's better than Guinness!'

I couldn't believe it when he asked me out, particularly as Mel was between blokes at the time. I thought: he's lonely; or he's sorry for me; or he's asking me because I can help him to get on at Brindley's. But as time went on, and he broke down my natural reserve and jollied me out of my occasional moods, I gradually began to revel in the halo effect of being in the company of such a handsome and charismatic man, of being the chosen one, the one he preferred to Mel. It also helped that Dad was tickled pink and, no doubt relieved that I'd finally shown signs of normality, encouraged the relationship along with barely veiled promises of promotion and a share in the company.

So I gave in to love, let it envelop me like an

anaesthetic; numbing me to everything but him. When Shane was around I couldn't drag my eyes away from him, studying the shape of him, getting close to him so I could breathe the same air, shivering in anticipation of his slightest touch.

The night he proposed I asked, 'What is it you see in me?' I wasn't being coy, I genuinely didn't get it. He studied me for a moment and then whispered, 'I see a lovely, extraordinary woman who has no idea how special she is.' And with those tender words I'd totally surrendered, my doubts melting away like a wax candle in sunlight, allowing Shane and his life-giving capacity for happiness to burrow so deeply under my skin that he became the best part of me.

Shane takes my hand and says, 'I know something's up and I'm not letting you move until you tell me what it is.'

I look at him seriously. 'We're going to have to do some temporary re-structuring for the next few months.'

'How so?'

'I'm going to work with Phil and the brew lab team for the next couple of months on the summer stout. It's important we get it right, and I have some ideas that I want to try out.'

Shane visibly relaxes. 'That's grand, Katy. Nobody better for the job.'

'So, I'm going to need you to take over as CEO for the next couple months. I can't run the company and develop the brew.'

Shane frowns. 'But I can't do the CEO job and run the EireWay project.

I extract my hand. 'Nobody expects you to. I've asked Peter Stanford to step into your shoes in Ireland. He's more than up to it now that you've done the spadework.'

Shane's face flushes deep crimson. 'Are you fucking kidding? You've gone over my head and given my job to a member of my team without as much as a by-your-leave. No way, Kate, it's not bloody happening. We're just about to land the contract with EireWay, and I'm going to be there when it happens.'

I walk over to my desk and sit down behind it. 'Sorry, Shane. Of course, I would have preferred to have passed it by you first, but you were in Germany, and I wanted to discuss this with you face to face.

Shane laughs bitterly, 'Call this a discussion?'

'Mel and I are going to Galway tomorrow for a couple of days to brief Peter and the team on the likely details of the contract and the PR campaign.'

'That's that then!' Shane heads for the door.

I call after him, 'I understand your frustration, but the success of the EireWay deal rests on us getting the stout absolutely right. You're the only person who has the knowledge to do my job and run Brindley's. I've made my decision and the Board have endorsed it.'

Shane turns and gives me a long, hard look. 'There I was looking forward to seeing my wife after all these weeks, but instead I find myself being given my orders by the boss!' He walks out, slamming the door behind him.

Blinking back angry tears, I switch on my computer and pull up another article about Rose Connolly. There are two photos in this one: one shows her working on a piece of jewellery and the other is a close-up of a delicate silver pendant with an intricate Celtic design. Her work is as beautiful as she is. I clench my fists, feeling my nails draw blood and an overwhelming, bitter flood of jealously gushes in, bringing with it the certainty that I am doing the right thing.

There's a gentle knock on the door and Mel walks in. 'I take it that Shane wasn't happy to have his wings clipped? He's just completely blanked me in the corridor.'

She looks uncomfortable and I wonder whether she's

regretting getting involved in our marital problems.

I shut the computer. 'I'm going to check with the guys in the brew lab and then go home to pack. See you at the airport in the morning.'

~

Saturday, 13 January 2018

James Cook Hospital, Middlesbrough, 11.55 a.m.

I sit in the waiting room sipping coffee while they attach Shane to a dialysis machine that will help to clear the toxins from his blood. Ben has told me that if the treatment works, there should be signs of improvement later today, and that I should try to rest. He pauses for a minute and asks me if I am feeling all right, and I nod and try to smile at him, feeling my mouth twist into a grimace. He hesitates, as if he is going to ask more questions, but his pager beeps twice and he hurries back into the unit.

I lean back, resting my aching head against the wall and listen to my pulse beating drum-like in my ear. My fingers restlessly twist and pull at the pendant I am wearing, and I remember, as clear as if it was yesterday, the day I bought it from Rose Connolly.

~

Wednesday, 25 October 2017—eleven weeks earlier

Rose Connolly's jewellery shop, Shop Street, Galway, 10.25

I stand outside the shop, pretending to look in the window. Mel has been in there for fifteen minutes and, by now, is probably Rose's new best friend. It is time to follow her in. I have had strict instructions from my sister: I can look round the shop, but I am not, under any circumstances, to engage Rose in conversation or let on that I have anything to do with Mel.

The shop is an assault on my senses: full of colour and

light, the air redolent of patchouli and freshly brewed coffee. My eyes flick to the back where I can see Mel relaxing on a sofa, nursing a mug of coffee and chatting to Rose who calls over, 'Can I help you?' Her voice is soft and her sky-blue eyes rest on me for a moment, friendly and warm. In the flesh, she is breathtaking, and I rudely turn my back on her, muttering brusquely, 'No, I'm just looking.'

I wander over to a display of silver and turquoise rings, each one more exquisite than the next. I hear Mel asking Rose how long the shop has been open and about Galway—what it's like have a business in such a vibrant place. Rose, in turn, asks Mel what brings her to Ireland. Mel replies, 'The Guinness and the men—in that order!' and they laugh. Mel asks Rose whether she can 'recommend a bar where I might find some fine examples of both', and Rose reels off a couple of names and offers to draw a map for Mel.

A sick feeling threatens to swamp me as I worry that Mel is being seduced by Rose, just as Shane has been, and I walk as far away from them as I can to a display at the front of the shop. My eye is drawn to a box which contains a miniature serpent, wrought in gold, each scale delicately carved, red rubies set in each eye socket, its forked tongue pierced with a diamond. I carefully lift the pendant out of its velvet nest and cradle it in my palm. It has the warmth of a living creature, and I dreamily caress its curves and undulations, the sensual feel of it under my fingers calming me.

As I walk back towards the two women, I hear Mel ask casually, 'So how did you meet him?'

Rose replies, 'Oh, I've known him all of my life. We grew up in the same town, but lost touch for a few years when he went to work abroad. I ran into him again last summer when he was visiting his parents.'

'What happened?' Mel is hanging on her every word and seems to have forgotten that Rose is the enemy.

'We started seeing each other. It was as if we'd never been apart, and ...' Rose smiles shyly, '... he proposed to me a couple of months ago.'

'When's the wedding?' The look on Mel's face suggests she is planning what outfit she will wear to the happy event.

Rose's expression becomes serious and she lowers her voice. 'Oh, not for a while yet. He's waiting for his divorce to come through, and we thought it would be better to wait until this one arrives.'

She stands and walks over to the cash register and I see the generous curve of the baby she is carrying.

'Oh, my God, you're pregnant!' The words are out of my mouth before I can stop them.

'Yes. Two months to go.' She gives me a smile that is serene and full of joy.

As I give her the pendant I feel a sharp, stabbing pain in my hand and see two puncture marks in my palm, oozing blood that is as red as the rubies in the snake's eyes. But it is nothing compared to the pain that I am feeling. Shane and I have been trying for a baby for the last two years, trying so hard that at times it feels as if our relationship has been reduced to a fertility timetable, efficient and joyless couplings and gut-wrenching monthly failure. Wordlessly, I hand over some cash and walk out of the shop carrying the rose-pink carrier bag embossed with her initials. In the street, I remove the pendant and carefully put it round my neck and thrust the box, the carrier bag and all references to Rose Connolly into the nearest rubbish bin.

~

Polly's coffee shop, Edward Square, Galway, 11.45

Mel finally walks through the door and I watch her make her way over to the table where I am waiting for her, refusing to respond to her cheerful smile. A cool drizzle coats the windows and I am grateful for the warmth of the open fire with its comforting smell of peat. Mel sits opposite me and orders a coffee.

I feel the sullen coldness of the snake hidden beneath my sweater and say, 'Managed to drag yourself away, then? I was beginning to wonder whether you'd decided to move in with her.'

Mel shakes her head. 'Listen to yourself! Surely it was obvious, even to you, that she hasn't got the faintest idea that he's spinning her a line.'

I snap, 'How do you make that out?'

Mel looks at the ceiling and heaves a sigh. 'Has Shane asked you for a divorce? Have you two stopped trying to make a baby?'

I mutter no and fold my arms tightly across my chest, hugging my resentment to me like a comfort blanket.

Mel settles back and takes a biscuit from the tea tray. 'Do you want to hear what I think?'

I grunt. 'I suppose.'

'OK. You're not going to like it, but my theory is that Shane has had a meaningless fling with the fragrant Miss Connolly, got her up the duff and he's flown into a blind panic. He's bought her off with the house and has told her he's married and is waiting for his divorce to come through—oldest trick in the book—and he's now sweating it out back in England wondering what the hell to do next. He knows that telling you will result in you flying into a blind rage and sulking for the rest of your moody little life, so he's between a rock and a hard place, isn't he?'

'Poor Shane, my heart bleeds for him,' I snap back,

and pick viciously at a piece of wool on the sleeve of my sweater, creating the beginnings of a hole. 'Sorry, Mel, I don't buy your theory and, even it is true, he'll be disappointed if he thinks things between us can ever go back to normal. When we get back tomorrow, I'm going to tell him I know about Rose and the baby and that they're welcome to him.' But, even as I say the words, I know they're not true, know that I will never willingly let Shane go.

Mel places her coffee cup carefully on its saucer. 'Well ... I couldn't blame you if you did that, but I think you should take some time to think it through before saying anything. Plus ...' Mel looks slightly awkward, '... if Shane jumps ship before we've secured the contract with EireWay, it wouldn't look good.'

I think for a moment, trying to put my head before my heart. Mel's right on both counts. Success in Ireland is likely to be followed by interest from other European countries and share prices will soar. I scowl at Mel and say, 'OK. You win. I won't say anything to Shane until the contract's in the bag.'

'Promise?'

I nod. 'I promise.'

~

Saturday, 13 January 2018

James Cook Hospital, Middlesbrough, 3.15 p.m.

A gentle touch on my upper arm rouses me. It's Kelly, the nurse who is looking after Shane.

'Sorry to startle you, Kate. I thought you'd like to know that the latest tests show that the level of toxicity in Shane's blood is reducing.'

I struggle upright and push my hair out of my eyes. 'Does that mean he's going to be OK?'

'He's young and strong, so there's every reason for

optimism.'

I moisten my dry lips with my tongue. 'Can I see him?'

'They're just tidying him up a bit. I'll come and get you in a few minutes.'

After she's gone, I pull out my mobile telephone and ring Mel. She tells me to stay where I am, that she'll be with me as soon as she can. I finish the call and shut my eyes again, my head throbbing as I relive the events of the past few months.

November 2017—January 2018

North Yorkshire

On my return from Ireland, I throw myself into perfecting the stout as if it's an antidote for my despair. There's an alchemy to brewing, and I am never happier than when I am working alongside the brewing team experimenting with new recipes, adding different flavours.

At home, the atmosphere is heavy with unhappiness. Shane and I don't see much of each other during the day as we're both frantically busy, but we still have supper together each night in the kitchen. Our largely silent meals are occasionally interrupted by his mobile ringing and he'll look at the screen, make an excuse and disappear for half an hour or so. When this happens, I put his dinner in the oven to dry out and sit and brood, asking myself over and over again whether I can bring myself to forgive him and try to get things back to normal between us. But the longer I leave it, the more impossible it is to imagine that ever happening. Shane looks haggard and unhappy and people at work start to notice and ask me 'Is Shane OK? He doesn't seem himself.'

There are a couple of weekends when he announces defiantly that he is going over to Ireland to 'catch up with the team' and I know that he is going over to see Rose. I spend these weekends in silent misery in the brew lab knowing that the sooner the stout is perfected, the sooner I can move out of this purgatory. In my head there is a cinema screen on continuous loop on which I constantly watch Shane and Rose, imagining them together. I am obsessed with them, consumed by them and sickened by them. But, I also long for Shane, long for what we had and love him every bit as much as I hate him. There are sad times when I want to give up, tell Shane to go and be done with it; mad times when I contemplate killing myself, or him. But Mel is always there, quietly counselling me to wait, to be careful, not to do anything stupid and I grow thin as the snake feeds on my unhappiness and fills the empty, childless spaces inside me.

~

Friday, 12 January 2018

Brindley's Brewery, Middlesbrough, North Yorkshire, 12.15 p.m.

At the end of our weekly team meeting, I announce that the new stout is ready and we walk down the corridor to the brew lab where a table has been set up with bottles of beer and glasses. I wait until everyone has a glass before proposing a toast.

'Ladies and Gentlemen, the results of all of our hard work: Brindley's Bittersweet Stout—the taste of an Irish summer. Please join me in drinking to its success, and thank you all for all your hard work.'

There is a moment of silence as everyone sips the stout, followed by spontaneous applause. Shane comes and stands next to me, slipping his arm around me, easily, affectionately, the way he always used to, and emotion clogs my throat. He raises his glass and calls, 'Thanks for everything, guys. I'll be back in Ireland on Monday to roll out those barrels. *Sláinte mhaith*!'

~

Middlesbrough, 2.30 p.m.

We leave the party whilst it's still in full swing. On the way home, Shane says quietly, 'Why didn't you tell me the stout was ready? I felt a bit wrong-footed back there.'

I snap back, 'Why didn't you tell me you are going back to Ireland on Monday?'

Shane exhales loudly. 'Katie, I'm not sure what's going on with you … we need to talk, there's something—'

I jump in before he has a chance to finish his sentence. 'Chance would be a fine thing. You're never bloody well around.'

Shane slams on the brakes. He turns in the driver's seat to look at me, his eyes dark with anger. 'What the hell are you talking about? When we started this project, you said I should be the one to lead it, to work with EireWay in Ireland. You suggested setting up a project office in Galway so that I could be on the spot and start looking for somewhere to base the production plant if we got the deal. And you asked me to act as CEO, which isn't exactly a nine to five gig!'

I look down at my lap and mutter, 'I just wonder whether it would be better if Peter carries on leading the roll-out with EireWay, so that you can start looking for other markets. He's doing well over there and—'

Shane slaps his hand onto the top of the dashboard, making the whole car shake. 'Why don't you just cut my balls off and be done with it.'

We sit in horrified silence for a moment, and I try to work out what to say next; what I can do to stop him going back to *her*. Finally, I say, 'I just think we need to spend some time together, get ourselves back on track.'

Shane looks at me as if he is sizing me up for a straitjacket. 'We've just spent the last couple of months together, and, frankly, Kate, we're so far off the track, I'm not sure where it's gone, never mind how to get back on it.'

'Just stay a week or two. Take a break before you go back.'

He doesn't miss a beat. 'I'm going back. There's too much that needs my attention over there.' He sighs and lowers his voice a tone. 'Look, Kate, I want you to go and see Ralph. I know you stopped taking the antidepressants because you were worried they might interfere with us trying for a baby, but he reassured us that they wouldn't affect our ability to conceive. You haven't been yourself for months, please do something about it.'

I stare out of the windscreen, struggling not to scream at him. How dare he mention my failure to conceive when his Irish mistress is about to give birth? How dare he speak as if I am the root of our problems? I feel as if my head is going to explode.

We drive the next few miles in silence, until we see Micklewell Crag looming ahead of us wreathed in black, rain-swollen clouds.

'Storm coming,' mutters Shane.

~

Micklewell House, 3.12 p.m.

By the time we get home, ice-cold rain is falling so hard that it bounces back off the ground and the wind is whipping itself into a fury. Shane drives into the garage, gets out, fetches a crate of Bittersweet out of the boot and goes into the house without a word.

I sit in the car for a minute, too battle-weary to move. But as the car cools, I force myself into action, and, as I lean over to retrieve my bag from the passenger footwell, I see Shane's wallet lying next to it, propelled from his back pocket when he got out of the car. I pick it up and my fingers snag on the corner of a photograph that is tucked into the back pocket. I pull it out and stare at it for a long moment. It is of Rose Connolly and a young boy who looks about nine years old. The boy is beautiful, with Rose's red-gold hair and a face that is the image of Shane. I don't even bother to cast around for an alternative explanation. I know that I am looking at Shane's son; know that all the time that we have been married, this boy and his mother have been part of Shane's life; know that my husband is a liar and a cheat. There is a ripping sensation inside my head, and I start to tremble. I feel as if everything that ever mattered to me has been ripped away: my husband's love, my hope of ever becoming a mother— my future.

A tiny, clear voice in my head hisses 'Do something!' and, without thinking, I get out of the car and go over to shelves on which we store engine oil, tools and such like. Tucked away on the highest shelf, I find what I am looking for: a white plastic canister of pure ethylene glycol which we use to stop the water in the outside lavatory freezing over during the winter months. I pull it off the shelf and pour a small amount into an empty jam jar, my hands clumsy in their thermal gloves. Once inside, I leave the jam jar on the kitchen work surface next to an empty bottle of Bittersweet and go through to the living room where Shane is sitting gazing into the fire, a half-empty beer glass on the coffee table in front of him.

I say, 'The drain outside the back door is blocked again. Any chance you could clear it before it backs up onto the patio?'

Shane gets up and I hear him go into the garage. I wait until I am sure he has gone into the back garden, then take his beer glass through to the kitchen and pour most of the ethylene glycol into the stout and stir it in with a teaspoon. I take a small sip, the stout tastes slightly sweeter, but

Shane has already had a pint and some nibbles back at the brewery and his taste buds will be slightly dulled. I take off my gloves and toss them into the fire, pushing them down into the bluest part of the flame with the poker until they ignite and become an unrecognisable, twisted mass.

Shane comes back into the room and I watch, emotionless, as he picks up the stout and swallows a mouthful and then another, draining the glass.

I say, 'I'm going to sleep in the spare room tonight.'

Shane barely glances at me. 'Please yourself.'

Before going to bed I go into the kitchen and empty the remainder of the antifreeze into the sink and run the hot tap for a few minutes to rinse all traces away. I put the jam jar and the teaspoon I used in the dishwasher and turn it on to its hottest cycle. I feel hollowed out; dislocated. I am like a ship that has been tossed into the eye of a hurricane. I know that I will have to battle my way out the other side, but, for the moment, I am spent and fall deeply asleep the minute my head touches the pillow.

~

Saturday, 13 January 2018

James Cook Hospital, Middlesbrough, 6.30 p.m.

I sit watching Shane sleep. He looks a better colour, and they've taken him off the ventilator. The soft hum of the dialysis machine calms me and, suddenly, for the first time in months, I realise I feel hungry. I go to the canteen and buy a sandwich and a cup of coffee. As I put my purse back into my bag, I spot the half-empty packet of Prozac and pop one out, washing it down with a mouthful of coffee.

~

Saturday, 13 January 2018—fifteen hours earlier

Micklewell House, 3.07 a.m.

Jagged sound pierces layers of sleep, dragging me to the surface where I lie, heart banging and mouth dry, straining my ears in the dark silence. My brain struggles to process the fact that I can't see the shape of the window in front of me until I realise that I'm not in my bedroom—our bedroom. Floorboards creak on the landing outside, and I sit bolt upright as I hear something being slowly dragged along its length. My heart leaps into my throat as I flashback to what I did last night, and I croak, 'Shane!', my voice hoarse with panic and disbelief. I catch a foot in the bedding as I struggle to get out of the bed and get to the door.

'Kate …' Shane's voice is distorted and twisted, as if it is coming from the depths of the ocean.

I open the door and hot shame washes through me as I see him, naked and soiled, lying against the wall. Whatever he's done, he doesn't deserve this.

He reaches out his hand and touches my bare foot. 'Sorry, Katie … not feeling well.' He retches weakly and a thin trickle of bile dribbles down his chin.

I rush into the bathroom and grab towels and dampen a flannel in warm water. I fall to my knees and gently clean his burning flesh, my loving, treacherous hands shaking, my sleep-clogged brain frantically trying to remember all I know about ethylene glycol poisoning. I fetch a duvet and pillows from the bedroom and tuck them round him.

He whispers, 'Thank you.' He is burning up, sweat popping up from his hairline and coating his face so that he glistens, other-worldly in the half-light coming from the bathroom.

'Don't move. I need to call for help.'

He catches my hand in shaking fingers. 'I have to tell

you something.'

'When I've made this call.'

In our bedroom, I call for an ambulance, and they tell me that it will take them at least a couple of hours to reach us because of the blizzard. I run to the window and pull the curtain back, recoiling in shock as I register the snow that is being whipped into horizontal sheets by the gale-force wind. There's only one road that will be useable in this, and I tell the operator that I will drive to meet the ambulance. She tries to dissuade me, but I am adamant, reassuring her that my Range Rover is up to the task and agreeing that I will ring back as soon as we set off so that they can provide advice should Shane's condition suddenly deteriorate.

I go back to the landing and slide my back down the wall until I am sitting next to Shane. 'We have to go. I'm going to get you dressed and down to the car. Get you to hospital.'

He struggles for breath and whispers 'I'm a dad, Katie. I have a son called Eoin.'

'Sshhh, it can wait.'

He presses my hand, his fingers so cold in mine that they feel as if they will break. 'Please Katie, I don't know if I'll make it to the hospital.'

I whisper brokenly, 'Tell me.'

'When I first went to Ireland last summer I ran into somebody I was very close to just before I came over here. I treated her badly, Katie. Told her I would be back for her, but I met you and ... and I never went back, never said goodbye. She had a little boy with her, and, I swear to God, when I saw his face I thought my heart would stop because ... Jesus ... he's the living image of me. Anyway, I asked her to meet me later that evening, and she told me that after I'd left for England, she found she was pregnant.' Shane turns his head and looks at me, his face contorted in anguish. 'I swear to you Katie, I didn't know about the boy, she never tried to get in touch with me!'

I hold a glass of water to his lips, and he takes a sip or two before continuing. 'We talked for hours that evening. She told me about Eoin, how he loves football, how he's doing at school; he's a clever little chap.' Shane looks up at me and smiles proudly. 'Over the past few months, I've spent time with him. He's a lovely boy, he deserves a proper dad and …'

Pain rips through me as I fall on my sword and say quietly, '… you're leaving me to go to Ireland to be with Eoin and Rose.'

Shane pulls away from me, struggling for breath. 'How do you know her name?'

'Your solicitor sent a letter here about the house in Galway. It was easy to track Rose from her address. Mel and I went to see her when we were over.' I pull the snake pendant out of the neckline of my pyjama top. 'I bought this from her shop.'

Shane stares at it. 'You've known about her all this time?'

'I know everything; that she's expecting your baby, that you've asked her to marry you and that you've bought her a house. The only thing I didn't know about was Eoin.'

Shane struggles to sit up. 'My God, you've got it so wrong. She's met somebody else, someone she grew up with. He's married, but they plan to marry as soon as he is free. He's the father of her baby. I bought the house for Eoin. Rose will hold it in trust until he is twenty-one, when it will legally become his.' He whispers, 'I sold my shares Kate, I'm so sorry.'

I say slowly, 'So all those phone calls, those weekend visits, it wasn't so you could be with Rose?'

Shane draws in a laboured breath. 'I saw Rose, but only because I was trying to get to know my son.'

I feel as if I have stepped off a cliff, my body hurtling towards the rocks below. 'Why didn't you tell me?'

He looks at me with eyes that are full of pain. 'Knowing how you long for a child? How could I hurt you in that way?'

~

Sunday, 14 January 2018

James Cook Hospital, Middlesbrough, 2.10 p.m.

Shane is as white as paper, but when I lean over and kiss his forehead it is cool and dry. Ben has explained that his recovery will take a while but that he will be OK. They're going to keep him sedated for a while to give his body a chance to recover. I am shaking with exhaustion, having had no real sleep for almost thirty-six hours and my head is thumping.

I walk back to the waiting room where Mel is sitting patiently. She has been an absolute brick, arriving late yesterday afternoon with a change of clothes for me that she has fetched from the house. We sat up all last night drinking tea and chatting, taking it in turns to keep vigil by Shane's bedside.

Mel smiles tiredly at me. 'Ready to go, Kate?'

I nod, and we walk out to the car.

On the way home I start to feel sick, and Mel has to stop the car three times so that I can stagger into the snow and throw up. By the time we get to the house I am so tired I can hardly string a sentence together and am grateful when Mel suggests I should go and lie down. I feel lousy and resign myself to a few days of discomfort while my body adjusts to the Prozac again.

~

Sunday, 14 January 2018

Micklewell House, 9.37 p.m.

A flash of light penetrates my eyelids and I slam awake as an almighty crash of thunder rends the silence. I lie for a minute, gradually registering that every part of my body is aching, and my headache has worsened. As I sit up, lightning jags across the room again and illuminates the shape of someone sitting in the armchair. I flick on the lamp, 'Mel! What on earth …?'

She is wearing Shane's towelling robe, hands hidden in the too-long sleeves, hood pulled over her hair so that all I can see is her pale, disembodied face.

'It smells of him,' she murmurs.

I feel a hot, prickling sensation at the back of my neck, as if somebody is rubbing it with sandpaper. Mel shrugs off the robe and comes and sits on the bed making the bedclothes tighten around me like a shroud.

I say, 'You're frightening me, Mel. Has something happened to Shane?'

She leans in, her face close to mine, her breath alcohol-sour, and whispers, 'Don't say his name.' She wraps her fingers round the snake pendant and with one vicious tug, rips it from my neck. 'When Mam died everyone tiptoed around you and your precious grief; your fucking depression. It was all about you. Nobody ever wondered how I was doing. I was eight years old …'

I touch her arm. 'Please, Mel …'

She shrugs me off and picks Shane's robe up from the armchair, draping it around her like a lover. 'And then you took him. The only man I ever really wanted. God only knows what he ever saw in you.'

Somehow, I find the strength to swing my legs out of the bed and take a few steps so that I can grab her arm and pull her round to face me, to say gently, 'Stop this now, Mel. We can sort this.'

She shoves me so hard that I fall to my knees. 'I don't think so. When I fetched your clothes yesterday I found the ethylene glycol. It was just where you said it was. Did you enjoy the tea?'

I remember the flask of tea Mel brought to the hospital; the sweet, sickly taste which she'd said was sugar to help with the shock; the way I'd blamed the Prozac for the headache and sickness. With a jolt I realise that this terrible tiredness is because my kidneys are packing up. Panic hits me like a sledgehammer and has me gasping for breath.

Mel yawns. 'I'm going to grab some sleep now. Then I'm going to see Shane. The hospital rang while you were asleep and said he's conscious and asking for you. I just hope it doesn't set him back too much when I tell him that you've taken your own life.'

I try to speak, but something is crushing my chest, stopping the breath before it reaches my lungs.

As she leaves, Mel drops the snake pendant onto the floor, where it glistens briefly before fading into the soft darkness.

My Law, Not Your Law

Mark Bastow

I wish I had never met her, that DS out of Leeds North
East Division.

She came in here as though we, the Calderdale lads,
were the backward lads. She rushed here, rushed there, as
though we were in the slow lane and she was overtaking.
Wasn't she marvellous? How did she cope? A single mum
holding down a busy job. I'll tell you how she coped. She
used other people. She spent half her time at work
organising the childcare for the wonderful Henry,
instructing her housekeeper, chatting with her ex-college
pals, booking theatre tickets and doing her Open
University course on living in multicultural communities.

The first morning she was here she asked me, in front
of Old Haskins, the Super, if I wanted to do the course
with her. I said being born on the Yorkshire–Lancashire
border, I knew everything about living in multicultural
communities. 'You are so funny,' she sneered. I could see
the Super wasn't amused by my answer.

Then there was my promotion to DI. The promotion *I*
didn't get. I suppose as a DS with great experience and a
great track record, I stood no chance. After all, *she* was a
line-of-duty widow, a single mother, and of course a
woman: three strong qualities to impress the female-quota-
conscious promotion board.

To make it worse, when she wasn't getting results, they
transferred me across to be her DS. *She needs a bit of help;
after all, she hasn't your experience.* Old Haskins told me that
working for Henrietta would help my promotion chances,
and that she thought a lot of me. I am not sexist or

anything like that. I don't mind working for a woman, but is it fair to ask a bloke to work for someone called Henrietta?

Then it happened: second morning I was assigned to her, as I was having breakfast in the canteen. In she waltzes, plonks down that ridiculously large handbag, and says, 'I want a word with you.'

I never like to talk with my mouth full. I like to chew my bacon well. It was that tasty streaky Brighouse bacon.

'You should try the bacon, ma'am. It has great flavour.'

'I'm in a hurry.'

'I never hurry my breakfast, ma'am. It's not good for me.'

'I don't like your sense of humour.'

'Not many people do. I admire your perception, ma'am: being able to judge my humour without hearing it.'

'Come on upstairs.'

'Yes, ma'am.'

She sat me down in her office and read me the Riot Act. She thought I wasn't responsive enough. I was surly. Me, surly? Her phone rang. It was Alison, her course tutor. No worries, she would meet her at six rather than seven. Now, where was she? I should get over my sour grapes because she got promoted. The board clearly thought she was the better candidate and, after working with me for a whole day, she could see why. Now, I had good experience. All I needed to do was get over the disappointment and pull my socks up.

Then she took a call from the nursery. Henry had a bit of a temperature. She then rang the housekeeper. No, Martina, the au pair, was in Sheffield today. Could she the housekeeper slip round to the nursery and take Henry to the clinic to see the nurse? Could she also make sure the gardener didn't leave any heaps of rubbish about? Now did

I want to say anything? Before I *could* say anything, she looked at her watch and said, 'Shit, I can't spend all morning chatting to you.' Then she was up and gone.

Next morning, the shout was to 11 Woodside Terrace. My DI was en route back from her mum's place in Doncaster. Poor Maisie Wigglesworth. Head bashed in. I met the Scene of Crimes Manager who was just extending the exclusion cordon the first officer attending had set. He was concerned that there was no sign of the murder weapon. Something like a baseball bat. He described the state Maisie was in.

'Bashed in passion?' I asked.

'Who knows? It was a ferocious attack. Multiple blows. Do you want to see the lady?'

'Not yet. Wait 'til the DI gets here.' Truth is, I hate looking at dead bodies. Who in their right mind doesn't?

I knew Maisie. Lovely lass. Good-looker. Real mixed up. Not a druggie or a slush, but just zany. Could be some man who thought she was an easy touch and found out she wasn't. More likely a woman whose husband didn't keep his hands and the rest of his anatomy where it should be. A woman like Mary Tucker, perhaps. I know most of the people in Woodside, and I knew Mary Tucker at number 13. Big-boned, muscular lass who used to go to school with our my sister. That was a year or two ago, mind you. Mary Tucker, I remembered, had a bit of a temper.

One of the gratuitous compliments my DI regularly threw at me was that I was a chancer, so I thought, *let's chance it*. I took a couple of uniforms with me, including PC Minnie Patel. I liked Minnie. She was good at her job.

We went next door.

'Hello, Mary.'

'God, it's you.'

'Well, I haven't quite reached that elevated status, but, if you remember, we were mates once.'

'We were never mates. Come in to the kitchen. You want a coffee?'

'Leave the coffee. You'll get one when the custody officer signs you in.'

That remark didn't upset her. I knew my hunch was right.

I cautioned her.

'Why did you do it, Mary?'

She just looked at me. She looked as though I had betrayed her. I supposed I had betrayed her. I should have protected her. Woodside people may have dirt under their fingernails, but they are OK.

'I can't believe you're still in the police. I thought they would have chucked you out years ago.'

'I did too, Mary. Now why did you do it?'

'You know why?'

'Yes, I do, but I need you to tell me. It's procedure.'

'She was humping Tommy. She had such a smirk on her face this morning. I went and got Tommy's bat. You know the rest.'

'Where is the bat, Mary?'

I heard something behind me. It was my multitasking DI.

'In the ginnel. In Mrs Robinson's wheelie.'

'Is Mrs Robinson number 17?'

Mary nodded. I felt sorry for her. She had been wronged by Maisie. She would now be wronged by the system. All because I betrayed her. She might have got away with it if I hadn't questioned her. I felt bad. Some crimes are best never solved.

'A word outside.'

I supposed 'a word outside' is the adult equivalent of a bollocking in the headmaster's study. I was right.

'What the hell do you think you were doing questioning her as a suspect? I am the SIO. I should do the questioning of suspects.'

'You weren't here, ma'am. It was all done according to the book. I cautioned her.'

'I am cautioning you.' She was interrupted by her mobile. 'Well, call the plumber. The number is in the book by the phone. And tell him I need it done today. And can you collect my dry cleaning? I need it tonight. The ticket is in the fruit bowl on the kitchen dresser.' Then, turning to me, 'You can take her back to the station and get on ringing round the restaurant and pubs in the Stanton case. Don't question her anymore.'

After I dropped off Mary with the custody sergeant, I drove over to Hanley's Garage. There was Tommy Tucker under the bonnet of a Land Rover. He watched me approach with that look.

'Well, you won't be bringing good news.'

'Maisie next door was murdered this morning. We've arrested your Mary. Sorry, mate.'

I had just sat down at my desk when the giant handbag plonked down on it.

'And where have you been? The custody sergeant booked Mary Tucker at 11.05. You now appear at your desk at 12.50. Early lunch, was it?'

'No, ma'am. It was police business. I am going for lunch now. Would you care to join me?'

She declined.

~

In the next few weeks, Henrietta mellowed a bit. She went from plain vicious to just plain nasty. It helped that she got kudos from the Maisie Wigglesworth case. Old Haskins said that the Chief Constable kept saying what a fantastic result Henrietta had achieved. Arrest made, and murder weapon retrieved within minutes of the DI arriving. He also said how kind she had been to let me go down as the arresting officer.

In these weeks, I also learned much about Henry. Not only were the daily one-sided phone calls with other mums, au pair, housekeeper, parents and others informing me of Henry's whereabouts, doings, goings and needs, I got it at home as well. Did I know that Henry was in the same nursery class as our David? Wasn't my boss so nice? My wife talked about Henrietta and Henry incessantly. She and Henrietta joined a salsa class with three of the other mums. Soon they were close chums.

I suppose Henry provided some interest as I struggled against the tide of muggings that overtook Sowerby Bridge. I say a tide of muggings. It wasn't that bad until the Chief Constable's mother was one of the victims. The Haskins strategy was to saturate Sowerby Bridge with police officers. The Haskins definition of saturation was three sets of uniformed feet on the Town Gate and adjoining streets and a couple of decoys standing around holding their mobile phones openly. Result was no muggings for the three days of the Haskins saturation and then condition back to normal. The main offenders were two hooded lads, sometimes on bikes, sometimes on foot.

It so happened I bumped into Joey North in his betting shop.

'Ay up. What's up?' he asked.

'A stable tip. Much Money, 3.40 at Wincanton.'

He looked at the screen.

'It's a long one, but so is life. Give it a try. How are things?'

'Got a new DI. Not easy.'

'I heard that. I also heard *you* were in the frame for that. I also heard that she's matey with the Chief Constable. You must be pissed off.'

I nodded.

'While I am here, do you know anything about two lads about twelve riding about grabbing mobiles?'

'No. Sorry, not my business. Do you remember Susan Bradshaw?'

'Not sure.'

'Lived in Maudsley Street. Number 6. The girl with the wiggle.'

'Yes. I do now. Fab hair. We all fancied her.'

'Saw her the other day with those two lads of hers. She lives here in Sowerby Bridge now down in the Avenue. Just in case you are interested, for old times' sake. She's single now. Expect you're still married.'

'Yes.'

'I thought so. You got that look.'

I went over to write out the betting slip.

'A hundred on the nose? We pay you guys too much. Come over here a second. Want a word. I'm getting a lot of heat from your guys.'

'That's what we do, Joey. We hassle crooks till we can put 'em away. You know the game. You know the rules. If you slip up, we grab you and put you away.'

'I don't mind the game. I don't mind the rules, but someone isn't playing to the rules. Your guys have turned up the temperature on us, turned it off on our main competitor who is now stealing our business.'

'You're saying the heats off Tomlinson's?'

He nodded.

'I'll be back to collect my winnings,' I said. And who'd have thought Susan Bradshaw would end up in the Avenue?'

Just in case you are interested, Much Money lived up to her name: 14 to 1.

~

The Chief Constable's dream DI was away on a command course for a week. The first day, I came in unshaven in our clients' uniform: white trainers, light grey tracksuit bottom and matching hoodie. Dressed that way, when four o'clock came and I went and hung round the rec at the back of the Avenue, I didn't look out of place. I had already looked up Susan Bradshaw on the electoral roll, she lived at number 27. She was clean on the PNC. Nothing happened that first day.

Second day, I got caught all day on an armed robbery in Halifax at the Piece Hall. It went into the third day, but I was back at the Avenue Rec by 4.30. Then Minnie Patel rang me. Phone snatch outside a fast-food joint on the Town Gate.

Down the footpath they came, two of them riding their bikes. The footpath was about a metre wide between two six-foot fences. I held up a piece of wood I found on the ground as though it was a spear. As they stopped, I grabbed them.

'Let go or I'll scream.'

'Shut up, or I'll punch your teeth out.'

They were two terrified peas out of the same pod. Fair-haired just like Susan Bradshaw. I wondered what she looked like now. I would find out soon enough.

I walked them down to number 27.

'What's going on? Who are you?'

'You'll find out soon enough. Go inside.'

I followed them in. Susan looked frightened.

'Do I know you?' she asked.

'You did once.'

'Were we at school together?'

'Got it in one. I'm police now, chasing two young lads on bikes stealing phones.'

'They wouldn't.'

'They would. Empty your pockets. Show your mum.'

Four phones appeared.

'Pick out your ones. Any more phones in the house?'

They shook their heads. I went upstairs. Found another ten phones in their room and a hundred and twenty pounds. It was a tidy room for a boys' bedroom. No sign of drugs or booze.

'You got a garage or a shed?'

'Out the back.'

A brick-built shed at the end of an overgrown garden. One thing was for sure. Poor Susan didn't have a gardener. The shed was clean, as far as I could tell.

'Send them up to their room.'

I sat down.

'Well, Susan, what do you want to do? I can get a car to take you all and book them, or I can say I found these phones in the bushes down by the rec. Can you control your boys, or do I do it by the book and book them?'

'I'll control the little bastards.'

'You'd better. Next time it'll be a caution; time after that, the court, and after that, you should know the rest.'

'There won't be a next time.'

'There better not be. I'll leave my card and on it I'll write down Minnie Patel's number. She's uniform. She's good. She's not heavy, but she's not soft. She can give advice. She can come and chat to the lads. Don't be afraid to ask for help. I'll leave that as well.' I put the £120 on the table. 'I found that with the phones. You obviously give them too much pocket money. By the bye, I always liked your hair. Glad you kept it the same.'

As I left, I turned and said, 'Make sure I don't see you again for at least another ten years.'

She smiled.

I hope that worked. I may have made a mistake. Hopefully, I have saved Susan Bradshaw some heartache. I walked in to the station with my bag of phones. Minnie and I started tracing the owners.

I got home that night and I was straight out again. A nineteen-year-old stabbed outside a chip shop in Outlane. They had taken him to Leeds Infirmary. We started taking names and addresses, statements and cordoned off the area for the scene of crime officers. Then it came through on the radio. Confirmed dead on arrival. These were tough streets when I was growing up. They are tougher now.

Next morning, I found out what a command course does for you. It makes you even more objectionable. The witch of Leeds North East was back and giving me earache. Why hadn't we rid Sowerby Bridge of the muggers? It's one thing finding some phones, it is another thing catching the muggers. This woman was some philosopher.

She was not impressed with me. I didn't seem to know very much. Why weren't the door-to-door inquiries for the stabbing complete? Well, they were nearly—ninety per cent—and we couldn't work through the night. Ninety per cent isn't one hundred per cent, and buggering off for an early night when a young man has just been brutally murdered wasn't professional. *I* wouldn't have called one o'clock in the morning an early night. We had done everything we could that night. Excuses, excuses, that was all my DI ever got from me. Wouldn't I have loved to push her off the top of Wainhouse Tower? When we were lads, we reckoned someone pushed off the top of Wainhouse Tower would hit the ground at 125 mph. Real raspberry-jam speed. Dream on.

We got the lad that afternoon. He presented himself at the police station with his solicitor and doctor daddy. Sixteen years old. He reckoned the other guy knocked into him in the chip shop queue. So there, take care in the chip shop. It's more dangerous than you think.

Next morning, I was having breakfast in the canteen. Tasty fry up, and in comes my persecutor.

The handbag landed.

'I want to see you in my office as soon as possible, but of course you don't hurry breakfast, do you? Well, eat away, and in the fullness of time come and see me.'

'That was wonderful, ma'am; just like Mae West.'

'What?'

'Didn't she say, "Come up and see me sometime?"'

The DI stood there for a moment, silent, and then spun round, grabbing the handbag, and marched off.

I finished my breakfast in peace and went to face the school ma'am.

'Did you pay a large sum of cash into your bank on Thursday?' Thursday was the day I paid a £1,000 from my bet on Much Money.

'Is it any of your bloody business?'

'I just want to ensure that Joey North isn't paying you.'

'You've got be joking.'

'Well, Reg Tomlinson reckons you and Joey are too close.'

'Tomlinson is a crook. You can't believe a word he says.'

'Tomlinson is a businessman. He may not be a saint, but what businessman is. Leave him alone. Concentrate on the real crooks like your mate North.'

Then the penny dropped.

'OK, ma'am. Message received. I obviously misjudged Tomlinson. I have North in my target zone.'

'Good. Perhaps we can get on together now?'

'Yes, ma'am.'

I was now a 'yes' man. Did what she asked. Behaved myself. I even dropped the horrible Henry off to his nursery a couple of times when she came in straight from home with him. I became a real brown-noser.

As I said, the penny had dropped. She came from Leeds. Where did Tomlinson hale from? Leeds. His brothers were still there. How did she afford the housekeeper, the au pair, and the gardener? Where did she live? I knew it was over Luddenden way. I checked. Six bed, six bathrooms, and a host of things you and I don't even bother to dream of.

I went through her desk drawers a couple of times when there was no one about. Not many DIs have Sotheby Catalogues in their desk drawers. She had a few items marked. Late nineteenth century maritime watercolours. There was an old birthday card.

To Dearest Henrietta. From Clare James.

That is *the* Mrs Clare James—the Chief Constable.

See you and Henry for lunch on Sunday. And congratulations on your promotion. The best woman won.

The best woman indeed! I suppose if I had a birthday card from the Chief Constable congratulating me on my promotion and inviting me to Sunday lunch, I might keep it in my desk drawer.

I started following her after work occasionally, just for the first half hour or so. Thursday evenings spot on 7.00 p.m., she would park in the multistorey Saver Centre car park. Same routine. Park on the second floor and then go up to the seventh-floor roof level. I parked over the way outside the Halton Centre and then I would run across to the Saver Centre. The hoodie was good. No one would make me out if the CCTV caught me, and I had the camera locations marked. One advantage of being a police officer.

Every Thursday evening spot on 7.10 p.m., Tomlinson would drive up the sixth floor and walk up and join Henrietta. Was it innocent? Could be just Henrietta using him as an informant. My nose said bribery.

~

I happened to go over to the Constabulary Headquarters in Elland Road, Leeds. An old friend. Chief Inspector.

'Forget it,' he said. It was the same over there. The Tomlinson family was off limits. You've got to smarten up. The old ways aren't good enough. Look at that inspector there. Him and his DS are the smartest ones on the block. Their money-management skills are second to none. Not like you and me, who take our salary at the end of the month, pay our mortgages, the electric and the rest, and then wonder why there's nothing left. They live in mortgage free houses, have Mercs in the drive, holiday homes in Marbella, and cash in the bank. As for Henrietta, she was the star turn. Everyone that was anyone loved her. She was the face of modern policing. She'd be back at Headquarters in three years' time as Superintendent. Try and rubbish her and everyone will say sour grapes on not getting promotion. Let's face it, you weren't the best woman for the post. You weren't even a woman. You need to wise up, knuckle under, obey the clichés and use this regularly on your nose. He passed me a tissue.

Driving down Commercial Street in Halifax one morning, I saw Henrietta walking into HSBC. It was a Friday. My first thought was: *thank goodness she didn't see me.* I was supposed to be elsewhere. Then my nose itched—bad. I'd had an idea.

I parked up in Cock Yard and slunk round to the newsagent opposite the nearest Barclays branch. Standing behind those postcard adverts, I saw her sneak into Barclays. A very furtive look up and down the street before she went in. Out she came and went down to the credit union. She used counter number four. Jane Madison served her. I watched Henrietta slip round to George Square and into the building society. I went back to the credit union and queued for counter four.

'Hello, Jane.' I put on my best smile. 'I need a teeny bit of help.'

'You need to see the manager.'

'Jane. Please help.'

Silence was the reply.

'Did Friend Henrietta ask you for a piece of cake?'

Jane looked puzzled and shook her head.

'Did she deposit cash?'

She nodded.

'About a thousand pounds?'

She pulled a face.

'A bit lower, say, eight hundred?'

'Seven-fifty,' she mouthed.

'Does she do most Fridays?'

She nodded.

'Did I ever tell you what lovely hair you have?'

Jane had her hair in a bob. Lovely cut. Suited her.

'Oh, push off.'

I pushed off. There it was. Fridays, she pays the money she gets on Thursday evenings from Tomlinson into half a dozen bank accounts, so no one bank sees excessively large cash deposits. Banks have to report large cash deposits that might be money laundering.

~

I had put up with weeks of listening to the adventures and achievements of Henry as his mother spoke to relatives, au pair, staff at the nursery and fellow mums. Weeks of being told how to do my job. I was convinced Henrietta was bent, but what should I do? Report her? If there was a cover up, I would end up in the shit. The system would label me as toxic.

I was out at The Weavers on the Burnley Road with Herself at a friend's engagement drinks. Old Haskins was there. We met in the gents. As he washed his hands, he said how pleased Henrietta was with me. Well, she successfully hid that from me. Now she wanted to help my promotion chances. She thought as I had been on the same patch a long time, a move would help. He said she was right. There were a couple of guys in Leeds leaving to head south to the Met. Things could move fast. Could be very fast. I could find myself over in Leeds working for a DI with a holiday home in Marbella next to Villa Tomlinson. I wouldn't stand a chance and all the while Henrietta would be doing the rounds of the banks every Friday with a smug smile.

Then it happened. It was the next Thursday. I was out questioning shopkeepers in the Halton Centre. In the toilets, I slipped into hoodie-ware and walked over to the Saver Centre. Up to the roof floor. Squatted in between a Ford and a BMW. Tomlinson was there first. Waited over by the southern wall, well away from all the parked cars. She joined him. They spoke for ten minutes. Then Tomlinson left. As he left, he stopped and looked my way. Had he seen me? Perhaps? This was getting risky. He turned and carried on. According to their routine, Henrietta would now wait another ten minutes before leaving. It was so no one would see them leaving at the same time. She stared out at the town.

~

I crept up behind her. I was afraid any second now she would turn and confront me. She didn't. She remained looking out on the town oblivious to my presence.

I crouched down. I quickly wrapped my arms round her ankles and lifted her up and over the parapet. I took her totally by surprise. She didn't even wriggle until she was on the way down. Sorry, it wasn't Wainhouse Tower, but it was the best I could manage. I don't know what speed she would have been doing when she landed in the closed alleyway below.

The next day she was found. The time of death was placed plus or minus twenty minutes. The CCTV showed Tomlinson's car leaving the car park in that time window. In that big handbag, they found five thousand in cash. Tomlinson's prints were on the notes. They found a burner in the DI's bag with a history of calls to and from a burner found on Tomlinson when he was arrested.

Crown Prosecution reckoned there was insufficient evidence to proceed to trial, but we all knew that Tomlinson did it. Didn't we?

So that's how I righted an injustice and got my well-deserved promotion. It may not have been justice according to the Queen's law; it may not have been justice according to *your* law, but it was justice according to *my* law. My law may be rough and ready, but it is quick and effective. She taunted me, she held me back, she stole my promotion and all the time she was corrupt. Now she has paid the price. I have no regrets. I'm just glad I did it before she had me shunted off to Leeds to work for one of her corrupt buddies.

A final note. What on earth happened to little Henry? He's playing in the front room with my David.

I never realised how close a friend Henrietta was to my wife. My wife agreed to be Henry's guardian and look after him if anything happened to Henrietta. Spooky, isn't it?

All men make mistakes, but a good man yields when he knows his course is wrong and repairs the evil. The only crime is pride.

~Sophocles

Vainglorious Bastard

Caroline Bale

Tim Shanahan found it hard to focus on the words he was reading aloud. A note had been left in his post box that morning which contained just six typewritten words:

YOU'LL PAY FOR WHAT YOU DID.

The note had unsettled him. As he scanned the audience in front of him, it occurred to him that the author of that anonymous note could be sitting amongst the sea of faces looking up at him—one of the two hundred gathered at the Dalkey Creates Writing Festival to hear him read.

Put it out of your mind, he told himself. *It's probably nothing.* He was honest enough with himself to admit he had trodden on a few toes along his path to success. Perhaps the note had been written by someone with an axe to grind, someone resentful of his achievement, who wanted to take the shine off his halo. A small-minded cretin jealous that his novel, *Vainglorious Bastard*, had been shortlisted for the coveted Man Booker Prize. A literary wannabe envious that *The Times* literary review had called him 'an extraordinary talent' and 'a writer destined for greatness'. That kind of praise inspired just the kind of begrudgery displayed by whatever coward had left that note.

He finished his reading and took off his glasses. The audience burst into rapturous applause. They loved his book; they loved him. He smiled and sat back, letting the adulation wash over him. Having an audience in his thrall boosted him, gave him a hit better than any narcotic. It was a scene Tim had repeated countless times over the past seven months, only the audiences were getting larger and larger. There were three other writers on the panel tonight, but he knew most of the audience had come to see him. Each of the authors had won some critical acclaim—and even success—but none had achieved the broad popularity he had. Without the kinds of sales he was achieving, none of them could be admitted to the ranks of writers of *importance*. As his agent put it, he not only had an abundance of talent, but he also had charisma. The two together were a highly marketable combination. He had already appeared as a guest on several television shows in the UK. For the moment, it was day-time television slots, but, after the Man Booker winner was announced, he would be aiming higher. He saw himself sharing the couch on the Graham Norton show with the likes of Ricky Gervais and Stephen Fry.

Coincidentally, he had read an *Irish Times* article on begrudgery on the plane on the way back from London only the day before. Apparently, the term did not exist outside Ireland. It was Irish begrudgery which allowed Bono to walk down Grafton Street unmolested, the article suggested. The Oxford Living Dictionaries had even identified 'begrudgery', as the article had done, as a uniquely Irish term, which defined a simmering state of resentment of another's success.

Tim fingered the note which he had carried around all day in the inside pocket of his jacket. No doubt there would be many more notes from future begrudgers. It was nothing more than a bi-product of his success, and something he would have to get used to.

The format for these events was always the same. He and the other authors on the panel would read from their work, and then there would be time for questions from the audience. Tonight, he was in Dalkey, his home town. There was a thrill to that, a sense of the triumph which he was relishing. Each of the four authors on the panel had their turn for questions, with Tim taking questions last. As usual, there were lots more raised hands for him than there had been for the authors that came before him.

Tim selected an arty-looking woman in her thirties for the first question.

'Tim, can you tell us where you get your plot ideas from?'

Dull questions like that irritated him, but he pulled his expression into one of interest.

'Good question. I was only discussing this with my publisher this morning. My plot ideas tend to land on my lap, often in the form of a eureka moment while I'm doing something else, like making toast or bringing out the bins.'

He continued on in this vein, trotting out his usual answer almost by rote. He called this one his 'just an ordinary Joe' answer. It usually got the audience on his side, made them feel that deep down he was one of them.

When he had finished, multiple hands shot up in the air again, begging to be picked. His mother, Olivia, sitting three rows from the front, actually turned around, taking in the dozen or so raised hands. Poker-faced. Rigid-backed. Her gaze quickly returned to his unpolished shoes. She looked irked. He could tell she was put out by his proving her wrong. He had made it as a writer in spite of her derision and scorn.

He had been surprised to see his mother in the audience. She still lived alone in the house Tim had grown up in as an only child, not far away on Vico Road. Tucked safely away from the outside world behind electric gates and eight-foot walls. 'Don't count your chickens,' was all she had said when he had told her the news over the phone about the Man Booker nomination. He hadn't bothered to tell her he was speaking in the town hall tonight. Yet, here she was. Happy to claim some parental credit for the talent she had so thoroughly denigrated his entire life. He could see her hair had been freshly blow-dried and her outfit and shoes looked new. Olivia had made an effort—not that she would let him know that. Her presence was the closest he could expect to a grudging acknowledgement of his achievement.

Four seats along, sat his wife—or, should he say, his estranged wife—Sandra. She had arrived late and had been seated by one of the stewards in the only spare seat in the same row as Olivia. As she sat down, he could see his first questioner appeared suitably delighted with his answer.

Next, Tim selected a bearded hipster, sitting in the second row, just in front of Olivia. It was always a good idea to take questions from a man at some point. It made him look like a rounded confident artist.

'The *Irish Times* has said your career could serve as a lesson in perseverance.'

A titter of laughter from the audience. Tim had seen the article, which described his rise through the literary scene as meteoric and which proclaimed him as 'an important new talent in literary fiction'. He wondered if Olivia had seen it. If she had she wouldn't have let on or she would have accused him of 'vainglory'. How many times had he heard that word as a child in relation to any achievement of his? Vainglory, the boastful or unwarranted pride in one's accomplishments or qualities. Perhaps that was why he had chosen to title his book *Vainglorious Bastard*? It was an accusation which, even still, had particular resonance for him. To win the Man Booker was the ultimate achievement for any writer, but for him it meant much more than the almost guaranteed income and financial security it would bring. If he won, he would finally be able to shut his mother out of his life. If he never again laid eyes on that judgemental face with its mean slash of a mouth, he would die happy.

The hipster continued. 'This is I believe the fourth book you have written but the first one to be published. Did you discover a magic formula, or did you just finally get noticed?'

Only a year ago, Tim had been coming to terms with being a 'failed novelist', having written three previous novels which had been rejected by every publisher and agent he had sent them to. Now his book was in bookshops all around the world. It gave him immense satisfaction to imagine all of those who had rejected him kicking themselves for letting an author shortlisted for the Man Booker Prize slip through their fingers. The hipster's question deserved his 'separate the wheat from the chaff' answer: the one where he remained modest but revealed the inner core of steel lesser writers lacked, and the strength of character necessary to finish what he started and achieve success.

'I am about to sign contracts on my three previous novels, so perhaps that answers your question? Writing is hard work; it is gruelling; those that succeed stick with their work, to the bitter end, improving it, making it sing. The magic formula to writing a bestseller, if there is one, is perseverance. Never give up, because that's what the begrudgers want you to do.'

The audience laughed as he knew they would. He liked to make sure he was keeping the crowd with him.

'Being a decent enough writer also helps, of course, which I hope I succeed in being … most of the time, at least.'

Tim noticed lots of eyebrows raising at his modesty; audiences, especially Irish ones, loved it when he threw that 'decent enough writer' comment in.

From his position on the dais, he saw Olivia throw Sandra one of her legendary frigid stares. His mother had used the fact of Sandra leaving him over a year earlier as a convenient hook to hang her long-standing resentment of her daughter-in-law on. The two had never liked each other.

Olivia was understated in an old-money kind of way. She looked down on anything or anyone she considered flashy. Sandra wafted in and out of a room in a haze of designer perfume to the sound of jangling bangles and the clicking of high heels. To her credit, Sandra had been supportive of Tim's early efforts at writing; however, she had become disillusioned after several years when he had so little to show for it. When she left, she said she couldn't go on with their lives on hold, waiting for a publishing deal that it was clear would never materialise. Now she was desperate to reconcile. It was too late for that. His life had moved into a new orbit, had taken a quantum leap. If she had supported him, she could have shared in his success, but she had made her bed and now she must lie in it. He had a new love in his life, the lovely Megan. Finally, he had met the kind of woman he was destined to meet. Megan was classy, beautiful and intelligent. She was a woman he was proud to be seen with, who would stand behind him, supporting him, encouraging him on to greater things.

The compère announced there was time for just one more question, and Tim selected an attractive young brunette at the back who was frantically waving her hand for his attention. Perfect. *Look and weep, Sandra.*

'The protagonist, Clive Mortimer, is such a flawed character; the way he treats women is repugnant and, yet, we are drawn to him. You've said before that there is a part of each character in the author.' The young woman's tone was teasing, almost flirtatious. 'Is Clive in some way based on you?'

There was a ripple of laughter around the room. He liked this woman's mildly combative approach. It made a change from the utterly predictable questions his fans tended to ask.

'I'm sorry to disappoint you, but I don't ride a huge motorbike or have multiple affairs with students young enough to be my daughter, if that's what you mean?'.

The audience laughed. Clive Mortimer, the anti-hero in *Vainglorious Bastard* was an unapologetic misogynist. There was a definite charge in the room now, a frisson of excitement. He was right where he wanted to be: in the spotlight, two hundred people— half of them writers— hanging on his every word. Olivia taking it all in.

'I suppose on one level,' he continued, 'there is a part of every man that is like Clive Mortimer or, if they were honest, that wishes they *were* like him. Clive represents an archetype of a man that dares not express itself in our current politically correct society. I think that explains the huge appeal of Clive as a character—he represents a kind of maleness that many men feel disconnected from now.'

The woman was still standing, microphone in hand. Not bad-looking. Great body. A face framed by masses of dark hair which tumbled around her shoulders. The attendant who had handed her the microphone was hovering awkwardly beside her waiting for her to relinquish it, but she looked like she had no intention of doing so.

'But not you? So, I take it the answer to my original question is 'yes'? You are saying Clive's character is based on you?'

The woman was definitely flirting with him. Several of the audience turned round in their seats to look at her, including both Olivia and Sandra. Tim smiled and sat back in his seat. He was enjoying himself.

'What I'm saying is that on some level there is an appeal in the alpha male stereotype, the kind of man who knows what he wants and takes what he needs. I'm not saying I condone Clive's behaviour, just that his character has appeal.'

'To men?'

'To men, and to many women, in my experience.'

Again, a ripple of good-natured laughter from the audience. He saw Sandra grimace. The woman sat down, she looked amused with his answer. He felt satisfied to have ended the session on a high note.

From the sidelines, he could see his agent, Roseanne Casey, standing and gesticulating with a cutting throat action to the 'compère' for the evening that the question session was to be ended. Now! The man obliged, and, taking the microphone from Tim, he brought the evening to an end.

Roseanne, a forty-something Irish–American based in London and one of the top agents in the UK, was a woman who demanded rather than asked for what she wanted. She was handling the requests for engagements and interviews which were coming in daily now due to the massive publicity around the Man Booker. There had been several approaches made about film rights and a bidding war was underway. That was where the real money was, according to Roseanne.

As he stepped down from the podium, Tim was, as usual, accosted by members of the audience looking for him to sign his book. Tonight, there were twenty or more queuing patiently, each one desperate to tell him about their own doomed-to-failure writing ambitions. It was half an hour later by the time he got away and, by then, both Olivia and Sandra had left. He looked around and couldn't see the flirtatious brunette anywhere. Fine. He was happy to take an early night. The Man Booker Prize winner was to be announced at a black-tie dinner in London's Guildhall in only three days. He needed to be relaxed, clear-headed. There would be many more interviews, appearances on TV. The stakes were huge. Last year's winner had walked away, not only with the £50,000 cash prize, but had sold more than 360,000 physical copies to date.

~

The following morning, Tim awoke alone in his flat in Blackrock and jumped up and into the shower. Today was a huge day for Megan, the fifteenth of October: the one-year anniversary of her husband's death. She was due at the flat at 11 a.m. The anniversary was a milestone. Megan and he had agreed that once the anniversary was past, they would make their relationship public. She would introduce him to her two teenaged sons with whom she lived in a fine terraced house at Seapoint, overlooking the Martello Tower. A house that she now owned outright, after her husband's life insurance had paid out.

Unfortunately, Roseanne had slotted in a last-minute interview for him at three o' clock in the Shelbourne with a journalist named Tania Richards so he would have to eat lunch with Megan and run, but he would be back in Blackrock by five, six, at the latest, in time to spend the evening with her.

He heard Megan letting herself in and looked at the clock. Ten minutes to eleven. He remembered where he had been at this exact time one year ago. He had left the flat in a hurry to catch the 11.05 a.m. DART to work in Dun Laoghaire. The job was a stopgap, a way of earning the money he needed to pursue his real career: his career as a writer. Eight years and three rejected novels later, at thirty-eight, he was still working at the same school of English, teaching spoilt Spanish teenagers, who had as little interest in learning as he had in teaching them. Sandra had moved out, maybe, three months before.

He had been running to cross the Frascati road as the lights turned red, when a motorbike had come from behind him down Carysfort Avenue at speed. He saw the rider break too late. Next thing, the powerful motorbike was on its side, sliding at speed a good thirty yards up the road, coming to a halt just short of the credit union. The motorcyclist bounced along the road just behind his powerful bike. His leathers were all that stopped him being skinned alive. Tim ran to where the rider had come to rest. The man was dazed but he was conscious. He looked to be in his late fifties. He told Tim his name was Jonathan Yates and he sounded well-spoken, educated. He insisted on sitting up in spite of Tim urging him to stay lying down. There was no blood. He seemed OK, and there had been no external sign of the injuries which were about to end his life.

The contents of Jonathan's backpack had spilled out during his fall somewhere back down the road, and he expressed concern to get his things. Tim remembered promising to find his belongings and getting him to lie down while he called the ambulance. Jonathan lay back down, his eyes closed. The Gardai arrived and quickly closed the road to traffic. One Garda squatted down over Jonathan, the other started taking details from witnesses who had gathered at the scene. Tim told him what had happened and insisted on waiting with Jonathan until the ambulance came. He remembered gently squeezing Jonathan's hand, a gesture of comfort and reassurance, and Jonathan squeezing and stroking his hand in return. It was a moment of intense intimacy between two strangers which he remembered with absolute clarity.

After the ambulance had left with Jonathan, its siren blaring, Tim decided to turn back and go home. He was feeling quite shaken, in no state to teach class. When he reached the spot where he had seen Jonathan come off his bike, Tim spotted a number of items on the ground. A MacBook which had been smashed to pieces, a mobile phone and, sitting on the bars of a drain at the entrance to a car park, an orange data stick.

Across the Frascati road, upstairs in his flat, he made himself a cup of tea and opened his laptop. He googled Jonathan Yates and the man's picture came up on the screen. Jonathan Yates, Professor of English at Trinity College. He popped the orange data stick into the slot. He had every intention of dropping it into the hospital later that day, along with the remains of the laptop and mobile phone. The paramedic had told him Jonathan was being taken to St Vincent's.

There were two documents on the stick. One entitled SYNOPSIS, the other, much larger file entitled MANUSCRIPT. He clicked into SYNOPSIS. It was a 600-word document outlining the story of a married Professor of English who falls in love with a student, setting off a chain of events that leads to his murder. It looked like Jonathan Yates had written a work of fiction based, at least in part, on his own life. He wouldn't be the first author to do so. Tim had written a character based on Olivia into each of his unpublished novels. Sandra had seen this as proof that he would never fully cut his mother's apron strings. Without his mother to hate, Sandra maintained, he would have to focus on getting on in his own life.

He read the first few pages of the novel. It was good. Really good. The writing was sharp. Lyrical. Jonathan's style had similarities with his own, but even Tim could see it was in a different class. It was the kind of writing Tim aspired to. The story drew him in and before he knew it, it was nearly lunchtime. As he was heating a bowl of soup, he suddenly thought of Jonathan and he picked up the phone and called St Vincent's A & E. Jonathan Yates had died in the ambulance—internal injuries.

Did he decide then to claim this stranger's work as his own? Looking back now, he didn't think it was right away, although the idea may have been forming unconsciously in his head. He just knew he needed to go to the hospital. It seemed the right thing to do. He was, after all, the last person to speak to the dead man. There had been a connection in the short time he had known this man, an understanding that was hard to put into words. They were kindred spirits, talented writers both, drawn together by fate. He had a sense of anticipation, like the universe was at last dealing him a new hand of cards. Finally, he might have a chance to get the payoff his talent and persistence not only deserved but demanded.

The hospital was where he first met Megan. He remembered the first moment he laid eyes on her. He had been directed to a room in the mortuary and, as he pushed open the door, he saw Jonathan's body laid out on a hospital bed, fingers already wax-like, entwined and arranged on his stomach. As he came further into the room, he caught sight of Megan. She was sitting alone at her husband's side, a flawless beauty with dark flowing hair and honey-coloured skin. He felt an immediate and intense attraction to her. He explained to her that it was he who had tended to Jonathan in his last moments. Without thinking about it, he found himself embellishing the time he spent with Jonathan. Jonathan, he said, had known he was dying and had begged Tim to make sure his beloved wife knew how much he had loved her. He had promised Jonathan that if anything happened to him, he would seek his wife out, that he would make sure she was not left alone. Her eyes, red from crying, met his and there was such tenderness there, such gratitude that he felt deeply touched.

Her accent was American—Californian, he later found out. She was much younger than her husband, he guessed she was, maybe, just a year or two older than him—forty max. She spoke at length to Tim about her husband. His love of literature, his work at the university. He had been her postgraduate supervisor. There was no mention of Jonathan writing a novel. Perhaps, like a lot of writers, he had not wanted to share his work until it was finished, perfected? Tim didn't mention the data stick to Megan, he just handed over the ruined laptop and the mobile. He drove Megan home and insisted that he would check in with her over the coming weeks to make sure she was alright.

He saved Jonathan's novel onto his own computer and set about changing elements of the novel, names, dates, places. Instead of being set in Ireland, in Dublin, he set 'his' novel in a fictitious city called 'Harovia', which, in his mind, was an amalgam of several cathedral cities in the UK he was familiar with, York and Lincoln amongst them. Some of the minor characters changed race, class and occupation, but the protagonist remained the same, bar his name. He cut and pasted segments from his previous novels describing weather and scenery. Finally, he gave his novel a new title. In his view, the changes he made, the sections he added in, were important: they added something significant. After several months, he had persuaded himself that the tone of the work had changed so much in his hands that it was primarily his original work.

He sent the novel off to several agents, the same agents who had rejected him several times over the past years. Roseanne Casey phoned him ten days later. She set up a meeting with her favourite editor who enthusiastically embraced the project. He found that the book only needed what he called certain 'jarring passages' to be cut out. All of the deleted segments were ones Tim had added, a fact which he simply refused to allow into his consciousness.

Within a month, Roseanne had sold the book at the London Book Fair for a six- figure sum. Tim signed a three-book deal with Hodder, his book was in the shops just six months after picking it up out of the drain on Carysfort Avenue. The rest? Well, the rest just happened.

In the meantime, he and Megan had continued to seek each other out, drawn together by the terrible trauma of Jonathan's death. When Tim gave Megan the opening chapter of *Vainglorious Bastard* to read, she loved it.

'You have a rare talent, a voice that needs to be heard,' she had told him the day after he had handed her 'his' manuscript. He was happy to believe her. When he looked at Megan, he saw his talent reflected in her eyes. It was intoxicating: her belief in him was everything he had craved and had not received from Olivia or Sandra. He found himself walking again with the swagger of his younger days. With Megan, his mother's scorn could be forgotten; he could finally be the man he was destined to be.

Now he was standing back at the spot where Jonathan had lain exactly one year before: at a lamppost outside the credit union, standing with Megan. She looked incredible in a fitted trouser suit which showed off her long legs. She had brought two simple bunches of white roses and gave one bunch to him. Together, they placed the flowers side by side up against the lamppost. They embraced, a sad, lingering holding. He could feel her breasts beneath her jacket, and he imagined himself entwined around her naked body like ivy round a mighty oak.

Over a rather hurried lunch at the Mellow Fig, Megan reminisced about the huge turnout at the funeral held in the chapel in Trinity a year before. The head of the English Department, Professor Laura Sedwick had phoned Megan that very morning to tell her that Jonathan was still in all their hearts and minds. Tim was feeling increasingly irritated with the continuing focus on Jonathan, but, given that it was the anniversary of his death, he had no option but to feign interest.

Megan was talking about some student who had

apparently contacted Professor Sedwick a few weeks before. This student had been in Colombia where she was studying for her doctorate in South American literature and had just heard about Jonathan's death. Megan remembered Jonathan speaking of her, a talented writer who he had mentored. Tim found his mind wandering. Lately, it had begun to really annoy him that Megan continued to speak about Jonathan. He had tolerated it until today, but once this anniversary was over he would have to put his foot down. Jonathan was past history; he, Tim, should be the main focus from here on in. He peeked at his watch, aware that he would have to leave in the next ten minutes if he was to make his scheduled interview in the Shelbourne. It was a nuisance that he had to haul himself into town, but the journalist had sold herself to Roseanne as having a big social media presence. Social media was king for Roseanne.

After several minutes, he realised that Megan was looking at him as if expecting him to speak. He had lost track of what she had been saying, something about having to move her two teenaged boys to a non-fee-paying school. While the life insurance had cleared the mortgage on her house, she really didn't think she could afford to spend so much of her remaining capital on school fees. In that moment, a way forward came to him, a way that he could establish a more favourable power balance in their relationship. Even though the fees in St Andrew's were, he knew, over seven grand each a year, Tim realised what he had to do.

'Megan, the boys shouldn't have to move school. Let me pay for the fees.'

Megan looked at him, her head cocked sideways.

'What, are you serious?'

'Perfectly. As you know I've done pretty well financially, and I think it's fitting that something positive comes out of my good fortune.'

'I can't let you do that; it's way too much ...'

Megan was protesting, he felt, just enough to look modest, but not enough for him to feel obliged to withdraw his offer. It was the right thing to do, and he reasoned it would ensure her loyalty to him.

'No, consider it done, and let's consider the subject closed.'

As Megan gushed thanks at him, Tim called for the bill, leaving a healthy tip for the waitress. He smiled; her reaction told him he had judged the situation correctly. By his calculations, paying the remainder of Megan's fourteen- and sixteen-year-olds' school fees would come to about fifty thousand euro. A substantial sum, but in light of the money potentially coming in from the film rights on VB alone, a paltry amount.

This was only the beginning for him, and he needed to ensure Megan's continued support. He had three previous books that Roseanne was in negotiations with on his behalf. It was vital, Roseanne argued, to have several more Tim Shanahan books in the bookshops to ride the wave from the Man Booker.

True, when Roseanne read the books, she had been brutal in her assessment. She pronounced the writing dull, the storylines weak, the characters not in any way developed. She had suggested employing a team of ghostwriters to help with 're-writing' these books using the style in *Vainglorious Bastard*. Outraged, Tim had stormed out of her office, slamming the door behind him. Roseanne had phoned later to apologise. Her tone and language had changed and there was no mention of ghostwriting. Rather, she was using the term 'radical editing'. The books were so good, she explained, that her 'editors' would be able, if given free rein, to turn them round quickly, getting the three titles into bookshops in time for the Christmas run thus leaving Tim free to concentrate on promotion. There was a fortune to be made. He had agreed.

He kissed Megan goodbye and almost skipped up the road to the DART for his next interview. He walked quickly from Pearse Station past Trinity College and up Kildare Street to the Shelbourne Hotel. The top-hatted concierge nodded in recognition and he strode past him into the sumptuous flower-filled lobby. He liked that the journalist had picked the Shelbourne to interview him. Nowhere else in Dublin had quite the same class. He had texted Tania earlier to say he would be a little late. She texted back that she was waiting for him in the lounge to the right of the lobby. He had frequented both bars in the Shelbourne over many years, but he had never actually been in the Lord Mayor's Lounge, a place he associated with affluent American tourists and old ladies. Or, if he had, it was after some ball at college and he had been out of his head and could not remember.

He recognised Tania Richards at once from the reading at Dalkey Castle. Her hair was different, pulled tight into a neat chignon, but it was her: the woman who had been asking provocative questions. She was sitting at a table in the window beside a roaring wood fire. The room was quite beautiful, resplendent with old paintings, antique furniture and, of course, masses of fresh flowers.

'I've taken the liberty of ordering afternoon tea for us both; you have to try the macaroons, they are to die for,' she said.

Tim smiled, took off his jacket and sat opposite Tania. He noticed now that she was wearing rectangular glasses which he was sure she hadn't been wearing last night. They made her look rather Scandinavian, a look which had always appealed to him. He imagined her whipping off her glasses and pulling her hair loose before they made love.

'Well, to my shame, this is the first time I've ever been in this room, so I'll take your recommendations.'

Tania cocked her head in an expression of mocked incredulity.

'You've honestly telling me you've never sat in this room, that you've never had afternoon tea here?'

What was it with this woman? She had a way of asking questions which was both flirtatious and accusatory.

The traditional afternoon tea arrived and was delicious. The tea had been served from silver-plated teapots into Royal Doulton china. There were different sandwiches, a scone with jam and cream and a selection of artfully decorated miniature cakes, including one of the pretty pink macaroons which Tania insisted he try. These had arrived on a three-tiered cake stand, sandwiches at the bottom, scones in the middle and cakes at the top.

He ate the feted pink macaroon, which, in spite of the sickly pink colour, left a bitter almond aftertaste, not at all pleasant. He took a gulp of tea to wash the taste from his mouth.

'But the final scene in the book was set here, surely?' Tania said opening a copy of *Vainglorious Bastard* and reading aloud:

> 'There were finger sandwiches with a choice of two fillings, a sultana scone with strawberry jam and clotted cream and a selection of miniature cakes, including one of the pretty pink macaroons which Sarah insisted he try. The dainties had arrived on a three-tiered cake stand, sandwiches at the bottom, scones in the middle and cakes at the top.'

As Tim scanned the room, he realised that indeed she was right. Jonathan Yates had written the café scene here. Tim had changed the setting from the Shelbourne to an imaginary café he had called Bella's. The scene in the book referenced the green chairs, the gilt mirrors, the works of art on the walls and the open fire. Sometimes he almost forgot that 'his' book had a previous existence.

He was starting to feel a bit nauseous now, not helped by the cross-examination he was getting. Tania was flicking now to another page of the book. God, she was keen. Too keen. Again, she was reading aloud. He would give her another five minutes, and he would be out of there.

> 'Clive Mortimer looked at his reflection. Known for his youthful looks, right this moment he looked alarmingly like a fifty-five-year-old man, which indeed he was. He wiped his mouth using one of the folded cloth napkins from a shelf over the sink which he deposited in the appropriate bin. He was feeling lightheaded, disorientated. For a moment, he found himself reeling around looking for the door to get back to his table. What is wrong with you, man? Pull yourself together.'

He poured himself a glass of water. He noticed his palms were glistening with sweat. Why was the temperature so warm in these places?

His head started to pound, and, then, he felt a razor-sharp pain behind his left eye, just as his mouth filled with saliva. He was going to vomit. He excused himself and made his way out into the lobby and down the stairs, making it to the toilet just in time to throw up. He splashed water on his face, noticing with some alarm how pale the face looking back at him in the mirror was. He wiped his mouth using one of the folded cloth napkins from a shelf over the sink which he deposited in the appropriate bin. He was feeling lightheaded, disorientated with a strong feeling of déjà vu. For a moment, he found himself reeling around looking for the door to get back to his table. What is wrong with you, man? Pull yourself together.

Joining Tania back at the table, he looked out the window at the street outside, the people walking by. He sat down heavily. Tania opened the book and started reading aloud from it again. 'Give me a break,' he thought; then realised that he had, in fact, spoken the words out loud.

> 'Joining the girl back at the table, he looked out the window at the street. He sat down. He doubted he would be able to walk as far as the taxi rank. His breathing was coming alarmingly fast and shallow.'

Tim realised he could not quite catch his breath. The pain in his stomach had intensified, and he clutched it with both hands. Tania was staring at him, but there was something about her gaze. Surely, she could see how ill he was, but yet she was smiling. He dropped his gaze to the safety of the tablecloth. Tania continued her reading aloud:

> 'His stomach was starting to spasm; the pain was like nothing he had ever felt. The girl leaned across the table and, whilst patting his damp hand, whispered over the starched linen covered tablecloth. 'Sorry about the pain; it's about to get a whole lot worse.'

He managed to look up from the table into her eyes. Her expression was cold, frigid. What had her words meant? If only he could think. He picked up his phone to call 999 but his vision was blurring, and he couldn't see the screen. Tania stood up and, while draping one arm around his shoulder, took the phone from his hand with the other. She bent down closer to whisper in his ear. He could smell her perfume, musky and sweet.

'Have you worked it out yet? The note in your letterbox? The book you published, it was mine. I was Jonathan's student. Before I left for my studies in Columbia, I gave him my novel to read. I didn't know he had died and when I heard nothing from him, no feedback, no encouraging words, I assumed he thought my novel was no good. I was crushed. Devastated. That novel took five years of my life, I put my lifeblood into it. Writing was all I ever wanted to do, but Jonathan's silence robbed me of my confidence. I buried myself in my work, focused on getting through one day after another. Imagine my surprise in Columbia when I came across my own book, online, four months ago? Different setting, different character names, even a different title, but my book. My book, that you stole from me.'

Tim looked up into Tania's face, realisation crushing him now.

'The macaroon? I've poisoned you, 'darling'. Just like my heroine kills Clive Donaldson. In about a minute your heart will stop, but I'm afraid I can't stay to watch. I'll leave you with this last quote,' she said, flicking to the end of the book.

> 'Clive Mortimer laid his head on the table; he was no longer thinking or breathing. Clive Mortimer was dying.'

The pain in his stomach was excruciating, he couldn't speak, or move but he saw Tania walk away. He needed to rest his head for a moment on the table. He hadn't enough energy to take another breath. His thoughts were impossible to hold onto, swirling and dissipating into a vortex of nausea.

Tim Shanahan was no longer thinking or breathing, Tim Shanahan was dying.

Doppelganger

Martin Keating

When Neville McCrum was called to the door of his house on the Malone Road in Belfast on the bright autumn morning of Monday, 8 August 1910, he found Detective Superintendent Kenneth West of the Royal Irish Constabulary waiting to speak to him. After brief introductions, Neville showed West into his study.

'Now, what is all this about?' he asked, taking a seat behind his desk. Neville thought it was always best to show public servants who's in charge.

West laid a document on the desk and pointed to it. 'Is that your signature, Mr McCrum?'

Neville Arthur McCrum. The name was his, certainly, but not written in his hand. The document was a personal note for fifty pounds, payee Patrick McGurk. This was inconceivable. McGurk, a prominent Roman Catholic publican from the west of the city, was someone Neville would never associate with, let alone incur a debt to.

It was absolutely absurd for West to have bothered him with this.

'I most certainly did not sign that.' Neville pushed the document away.

'The description of the man who did resembles you very closely, sir.'

From the drawer of his desk Neville produced an example of his proper signature. 'There, see. Now you haven't told me what this is about, Superintendent.'

'A gambling debt,' said West, folding the document and returning it to his inside pocket.

'I don't gamble,' Neville replied stiffly.

'I didn't imagine you did, sir.' West said, a hint of condescension in his manner, 'In any case, gambling debts are not enforceable.'

'Then what in blazes are you doing here?'

'I came to advise you that someone is going around the city impersonating you, sir. But don't worry, we'll catch up with him.'

Neville was angrier with the Chief Superintendent than the imposter. Why have all this early morning drama on his doorstep, when West could have simply called to the office?

'See that you do,' Neville said, dismissing the policeman.

~

The news about the imposter was, certainly, an annoyance but flattering, in a way. Who would not want to be Neville McCrum? Belfast's commercial lion. Under Neville's guidance the McCrum textile and light engineering businesses had become one of the top-ranking enterprises in the city. His daring and acumen had enriched the McCrum family trust, to which all profits accrued, and which supported the entire, extended, McCrum family. Neville resented the trust and the watertight terms of its deed. Why should he have to share the fruits of his genius with the other members of the family—a bunch of talentless and vapid hangers-on?

As the autumn months passed, family was much on Neville's mind. He was forty-three, at the height of his powers and thinking it was time to father an heir and establish his own dynasty. His previous plans had envisaged contracting a marriage by May 1917, when he would turn fifty—an age at which a man still enjoyed his full sexual potency. However, that summer, Dulce, third daughter of Sam McKinley, the shirt maker, had caught his eye. Modest in bearing and never forward in speech, she was, even at fourteen, a broad-hipped and busty girl, likely to make excellent breeding stock. He had an understanding with Sam McKinley that, when Dulce reached sixteen, he might begin to court her. Neville expected that their attachment would be quite something for McKinley—who was very much in the second rank of the city's businessmen—to boast of.

Dulce should make a better fist of motherhood than Neville's sister, Flora, who was at her wit's end because of her son Alexander's extravagance and degenerate way of life. Neville —as head of the family trust—had been obliged to cut off finances to the pair of them, news which had sent Flora, in a state of nervous collapse, to a sanatorium in the Antrim hills. From where she pleaded with Neville to find Alexander and bring him home, the wastrel having last been seen on the French Riviera.

Therefore, in late November 1910, armed with a stern sense of sibling duty, Neville McCrum set out for Nice.

~

Le Grand in Nice was the first casino that Neville McCrum had ever visited. Had he not been on the trail of his sister's dissolute boy, he would never have found himself in such a house of sin. Once inside, he observed the patrons and the games with his usual cold analytic intensity. Gifted with a quick mind and fantastically retentive memory, Neville soon grasped the essentials of the card game that the Americans call blackjack and the French vingt-et-un. Playing with a businessman's cool calculation rather than the gambler's élan, he was soon winning considerable amounts.

His prowess at the tables aroused admiring attention, particularly from the opposite sex. Which was no more than his due, Neville felt, he being a vigorous man in his prime, endowed with those qualities women covet in particular: money, success and charisma.

One fateful evening, as Neville was about to mount the steps to the casino, a figure bumped against him. He was about to remonstrate at the rudeness, when he saw that it was a young woman, quite beside herself and crying. She leaned an arm on his shoulder and buried her head in his chest.

'Ah,' she exclaimed, 'I shall die. I shall die this night.'

'Whatever is the matter, mademoiselle?' Neville asked.

She lifted her face towards his. 'Tonight, I have had the most terrible news.'

He had never seen such blue eyes and such a perfect mouth, albeit the eyes were red with tears and the mouth distended in distress. Her beauty moved him to console her. 'Well, you should sit down and have a brandy,' he advised.

He brought her to the salon in the casino and ordered brandies. Once seated, she wept without pause. Neville cautiously extended a hand to pat her on the shoulder. 'Mademoiselle, please.' They were attracting attention, and Neville feared he might be thought the cause of his companion's distraught behaviour.

She lifted her head and sniffled. 'Madame. Or, at least, it was until tonight.'

An abandoned female, and a hysterical one to boot! Perhaps a waiter would arrange for a taxi. 'Well, we must get you home, madame,' he said.

'I have no home, I have nothing anymore. Only death. Only death.'

Now thoroughly alarmed, Neville half-rose, to go find help. Her hand reached out and caught his wrist.

'Only death, m'sieur. Tonight, my husband suicided.'

Neville attempted gently to release himself from her firm grip, while trying to attract the attention of the white-coated waiters who looped past, faces averted.

'I'm sorry, I am causing such a scene. Please stay,

m'sieur, I will be calm, but I need someone to talk to, or I too will go the way of my poor Guillaume.' She straightened in her seat but did not release his wrist. 'Please sit with me. Please.'

Neville listened distractedly as she told her story of grief. She was Sylvie Auteuil and her husband, Guillaume, a wounded veteran of the French colonial wars, had shot himself that very evening.

'Guillaume was a great man, a war hero. To see him in uniform, m'sieur! He was captured by the Tuareg and they made us to pay a large ransom. But they are devils in human form, m'sieur, and, before releasing Guillaume, they deprived him of that which makes a man a man. The shame of that mutilation slowly destroyed his will to live. So sad, m'sieur.'

A calm had descended over her, making her beauty even more transcendent. The brandies arrived, and Sylvie wondered if she might have something to eat—she was feeling faint from grief.

Later in the cab, as he took her home, she lay her head against Neville's shoulder. 'You have been so kind to let me tell you my troubles.' She closed her eyes and sighed, reaching for his hand and squeezing it. Such strength in those thin arms. 'I feel that I have found a friend for life, m'sieur. But you haven't told me your name.'

'I am Neville Arthur McCrum, from the Malone Road in Belfast in the United Kingdom of Great Britain and Ireland.'

'Ah, you are the famous Irish gentleman I hear about who is causing such a stir,' she replied in a honeyed voice, 'and you make such a fuss over poor me!'

On her doorstep, her lips brushed against his cheek as she asked him to call on her again. 'You have saved my life, Monsieur Neville Arthur McCroomb. Now it belongs to you.'

Over the next days, Neville witnessed Sylvie recovering her joie de vivre, blossoming under his dynamism and charisma. When she smiled, it sent a jolt through Neville's body as if he had touched a bare electric wire. She had lustrous chestnut hair, perfect skin and intelligent deep blue eyes, which never wavered from his face as she listened to him, spellbound. She had an insatiable thirst to hear of his achievements; the new machines he had invented, the processes he had streamlined, the doubling of profits every four years—at which her eyes went wide and filmed over with emotion.

'Ah,' she said, 'how wonderful it all sounds. You must be exceedingly rich, Neville?'

A chagrined Neville told her that the wealth belonged to the family trust as a whole and not the individual family members.

'And have you a large Irish family, no?'

'Actually, there are quite a few of us. There are over a score of dependents on the trust.'

'So many! Poor you. No wonder you need to make a recreation.'

Neville explained that he was not on holiday but searching for his sister's son.

'You are so considerate to make this quest to redeem your nephew. I think I might have met him once; he seemed to me a troubled young man. This trust is big enough for everyone, no?'

~

Neville kept his promise to be home by Christmas—and not to return alone. He brought Sylvie with him when he visited Flora, as well as the news that the trust was unable to continue paying for her rehabilitation. Before leaving Nice, he had sent a cable to Sam McKinley informing him that Dulce was now out of the running in the marriage stakes. ALL BETS ARE OFF, the cable read. Neville thought that a witty touch, given the circumstances of his first sighting of Sylvie. As to Alexander, well, once Neville encountered his bride-to-be, the little parasite had been entirely banished from his thoughts.

The first week of January 1911 saw Detective Superintendent West again at his door. 'We arrested the imposter over the Christmas holidays and he's now in Crumlin Road jail. I thought you might care to look him over.'

'Why ever should I want to do that?' Neville said.

'He bears quite a striking resemblance to you.'

'I have other things to do than gape at criminals, Superintendent.'

'No doubt you're happy that we've caught him.'

'It's your bloody job to catch him. I wonder that it took you so long. Now was there anything else, Superintendent?' Neville asked.

'No, sir. That was all.' West looked crestfallen.

'I've no doubt that there are other criminals out there in need of catching. Don't let me detain you.'

~

The wedding of Neville Arthur McCrum and Sylvie Christine Auteuil was held in early March and declared by the *Belfast Telegraph* to be a spectacle on a par with a royal visit. Neville revelled in the admiring and envious glances directed towards his beautiful wife. 'You surprise me so much, chéri,' she whispered as they sat at the head of the banquet table. 'Usually a woman has the pride to plan her own wedding, but I could never have bettered this splendid occasion. You are so accomplished, Monsieur Neville Arthur McCroom.'

'I can master anything, in any field, that I set my mind to,' Neville boasted contentedly, 'I set out to get you, and I got you. And now you will give me the most wonderful children.'

'Ah.' Sylvie said. And then 'Ah' again.

She looked in Neville's eyes and took his hand and pressed it between hers. 'I remember you saying to me, so often, that with me alone your life is complete. Yes.'

'Yes,' Neville said, seeing the first cloud encroaching on the sunny uplands of their life ahead.

'Mon chéri,' she said, with a little moue, 'all our love has to be for just us. Before I married Guillaume, my doctor advised that for me to fall enceinte is a death sentence. I cannot carry a child; neither it nor I will survive.'

'You never said,' Neville protested.

'Guillaume, sweet man, accepted it. And, as a woman I found I could not speak of this tragedy. I would gladly make the sacrifice for you, chéri, but if I die how can you bear the loss?

'I should understand if you would wish a divorce, after a suitable period,' Sylvie, continued, her eyes moist. 'Though disappointed, I would not think you too very cruel.'

Well, there most certainly was not going to be any divorce. Neville cursed his impetuous departure from his well-laid plans, under the influence of the Mediterranean sun and her heady perfume. In calm temperate Belfast, he realised his mistake, but to make the whole town aware of his foolishness? He could hear the sniggers at his expense, at his club and in the lodge meetings. Divorce would make his situation a hundred times worse. 'You ought to have told me,' he said, 'but, since you didn't see fit to do so, I'll have to make the best of it, won't I?'

'You are such a fine man.' She kissed him warmly, and throughout their chaste honeymoon fortnight, she frequently and tearfully praised his noble nature.

Neville thought it best—when they returned to Belfast—that they maintain separate bedrooms.

'Ah, chéri, you are so thoughtful,' Sylvie said, 'it is torture for me to be so near you when we are unable to requite our loving urges.'

~

The frustrations in Neville's life seemed to fire his creativity. In April of 1911, he invented a gearing system that allowed each operator in the factory to control twenty looms and run them non-stop for twenty-three hours each day. The dismissal of two hundred workers and the resulting thirty per cent increase in profits—which a year before would have had him whistling in the corridors—barely pierced the gloom that surrounded him.

In April also, the imposter was tried and sentenced to a year's hard labour.

Sylvie set out to become close friends with Flora, and Neville's sister was soon again a frequent visitor to Malone Road. Neville welcomed the development, as relations between the siblings had suffered further after his nephew's return home. Alexander had been imprisoned in Marseilles, where he had been obliged to perform arduous and unspecified tasks for the matelots also incarcerated there. He had come back much embittered, not only towards Neville, but towards his mother also.

Throughout the summer and autumn, Neville continued to scale new heights of success. In December it was announced that he was to be knighted. His name had been proposed by Arthur Balfour, the leader of the Conservative and Unionist Party. There was great rejoicing at his masonic lodge. Yet another accomplishment to be proud of.

Sylvie greeted the news with a great shriek of joy. 'I shall be most humbled to meet the King, and, of course, the Queen,' she enthused.

'You're not invited, Sylvie,' he told her. He had no intention of taking her, as, frankly, she did not deserve it.

Finding her hour in the spotlight so abruptly and finally torn from her grasp, Sylvie sent a whiskey decanter whistling past Neville's ear. Flora came to tell him what a terribly hurtful thing he had done to his wife. He responded that the honour was his, his alone, for what he had contributed, and proceeded to deliver some home truths to Flora, concerning her never having done anything except to eat cream cakes and beget a prodigal. His candour sent his sister wailing home—down the length of the Malone Road—loud as the factory siren.

Christmas and the 1912 New Year passed in tense silence. Neville was to be knighted in the first week of February and, to avoid further unpleasantness, he decided to spend the week before the ceremony in London. As the boat left Belfast and the lights of the city faded into the mist, Neville felt an unprecedented stab of utter loneliness, and, proud man though he was, he could not staunch the flow of tears.

'Is it you, Mr McCrum?' he heard a soft female voice ask. 'The salt air makes my eyes sting too.'

It was Dulce McKinley. In just eighteen months, she had developed remarkably, now almost as tall as him and truly voluptuous. Dulce was going to London to start an apprenticeship to a couturier. Full of life and plans and wanting to experience everything. And her youth and daring infected Neville too. They spent a whirlwind week together, dinners in the best restaurants, musical theatre, concerts, culminating in a heedless twilight embrace in Green Park by the Wellington Arch, where Neville, in urgent retreat, had left some stuff on her petticoats. 'Accidents will happen, Mr McCrum,' Dulce told him, 'even to the most perfect of us.'

This was life as it was meant to be; not the living death of his marriage. Dulce was the one he should have made his. If he'd only been patient, look how perfectly she had turned out. She hung on his every word, she was perfectly complaint to his wishes. And such a figure.

~

Damn it, damn it, damn it. Dulce was with child. You had only to look sideways at any of the McKinley girls and they'd blow up like bladder wrack on a sunny beach. The tiny drop of seed Neville had left behind in their tryst had pounced on one of her eggs. There was clearly no margin for error when a man gifted with such potent, hard-swimming fellows came in close proximity to a girl as fecund as Dulce McKinley.

This would be difficult and expensive.

Sir Neville wrote a note to Dulce expressing surprise and commiseration at the news, carefully avoiding any admission of paternity or explicit offer of financial support.

Doubly difficult and expensive.

The stupid McKinley girl wrote to Flora. 'Pouring her heart out to me,' Flora asserted in a penny-novella tone.

Damn and double damn. Whatever happened to womanly shame?

Triply difficult and ruinously expensive, now that Flora, his woolly sheep of a sister, had told Sylvie, also showing her Dulce's letter.

'Cruel Monsieur Sir Neville Arthur McCroom, such filthy business with a child,' Sylvie cried with a mercenary gleam in her eye. 'I think now, you give me what is mine without your sins being told in public, no?'

They were ganging up on him, without thought of propriety, loyalty to the sacred vows of marriage, or the bonds of family. Dulce, no virgin she, and a fine ally for his manipulative wife. As for his feeble-minded sister, full of spite over her stupid son. Sir Neville McCrum, a man of unexampled enterprise and towering genius, would be paraded through the town like a mangy tomcat in a cage.

They imagined they had him in their grip, with no

escape except shame and penury. Well, Sir Neville McCrum had been tested by Fate before and by cleverer people than those three harpies.

~

He might be looking in a mirror. The figure emerging shakily from Crumlin Road prison, even with the beard, was truly Sir Neville's doppelganger.

'You there, I want a word.'

The man, who had been looking at the sky in a wistful way, recoiled in fear. 'Ah, now mister, I don't want trouble. I've paid my dues, so I have.'

'Name? Answer me.'

'Walter Craig, so it is.'

'You're a Belfast man?'

'Aye.'

'A Protestant?'

'Aye and proud of it.'

'In that case, I am prepared to help you, brother.'

'Oh, aye?' The confidence trickster looked at Sir Neville with an appraising air. 'We certainly do look like two peas in a pod.'

'Have you repented of your past, brother?' Sir Neville asked, keeping his manner strict.

'Aye. And embraced my saviour, Jesus Christ. I was just thanking the Lord for my first breath of free air, when you came up there, so I was.'

~

Sir Neville had paid for a fortnight's lodgings in a city hostel. At the table in the sparse room, he explained that it was his Christian duty to forgive Walter, but only if Walter freed himself forever of his past life of sin. Which he would do by confession and renunciation and Sir Neville would pay him ten shillings for each session.

'Would it be possible to get an advance now, Mr McCrum? For to get some clothes and other things I need to find work.'

'You haven't worked a day in your life, Craig. All you crave is the devil's buttermilk.'

'No, never, Mr McCrum.'

'You will get your money only if you make a full disclosure of your iniquities. Do I have your promise?'

When Craig nodded, Neville took a bottle of Bushmills from his satchel and set it on the table.

'Oh, you're God's only gentleman, so you are Mr McCrum.'

So began the week of confessions, in the course of which Sir Neville learned all one might need to know about creating a new identity and fooling all manner of officials and staunch citizens. Sir Neville, with his retentive memory, did not need to take notes and Walter, aided by the whiskey and the fact that nothing being committed to paper, gave a frank account of himself. He was as proud of his accomplishments—meagre and despicable as they were—as Sir Neville was of his many successes.

At the end of the week, Sir Neville gave Walter five pounds along with some of his own linen and suits—worn but still serviceable. 'You will set out on a new path from this day on, Craig.'

'You're very generous to me, your honour.'

'And I will be more so, Craig. I will give you a passage to America, where you may make a new start in life.'

'Oh, that's wonderful, so it is.'

'You have put your disreputable past behind you, and therefore it is my duty to set you on your feet again. Come to my house on Sunday evening, with your travel papers in order and I will have a ticket ready for you. No foolishness, now, Craig. No impersonations—the papers in your own name.'

Craig wept. He clutched Sir Neville's hand and dropped tears on it.

That evening, Sir Neville travelled to Stranraer as Walter Craig, making sure to be remembered there, by having his name taken by the local police. Two days later—after a brief sojourn in London—and once again Sir Neville McCrum, he crossed from Liverpool to Dublin and returned to Belfast.

When the doorbell rang to announce Walter Craig's arrival at eight o'clock on Sunday evening, Sir Neville answered the door himself—the maid lay bludgeoned on the kitchen floor and Sylvie was already dead and laid her out on her bed.

Walter too succumbed to few well-aimed strikes to the head.

Earlier that day Neville had made a visit to Flora, on the pretext of apologising but, in reality, to steal a fire iron from his nephew's room—which he used to kill his three victims, throwing it, complete with Alexander's fingerprints, into the bushes by the front path. Before he left the house, he turned on the gas and left a lighted candle in the hall. The fire would burn the flesh from the bodies—especially Craig's tell-tale fingerprints—and seem just the sort of attempt at concealment that an idiot like Alexander would make.

Neville would have gladly thrown Dulce McKinley on the pyre too, had he been able to find a plausible pretext for luring her to the house. Still, even with his silly sister's help, the trollop would have a hard time getting the McCrum trust to pay for her bastard. It pained him to leave a fortune behind, but he had learned the hard way what poor outcomes following his emotions led to. He had to disappear completely, and, if keeping his life meant sacrificing most of his wealth, so be it. As Walter Craig, reborn in America with a clean slate, he would make a fortune all over again—an even greater one thanks to his genius and ruthless pragmatism.

He took the morning train to Dublin where he had a tailor sew into the lining of his suit, the diamonds and gold pieces—to the value of two thousand pounds—that he had recently obtained in London. At Kingsbridge, he entrained for Cork and the transit port of Queenstown. Ahead of him, a glorious future. America. Freedom. Destiny.

At twelve noon, on 11 April 1912, after a short transfer by lighter from Queenstown to the anchorage at Roche's Point, he boarded the transatlantic liner that would take him to New York. Standing at the rail watching the last of Europe receding into the haze, Neville Arthur McCrum experienced an overwhelming feeling of invincibility. The cleverest man in Creation (and always a proud Belfast man), standing on the deck of RMS Titanic, the finest vessel ever built by humankind and the crowning achievement of his beloved native city.

There is a holy love and a holy rage, and our best virtues never glow so brightly as when our passions are excited in the cause. Sloth, if it has prevented many crimes, has also smothered many virtues; and the best of us are better when roused.

~Charles Caleb Colton

The Apology

Adrian Taheny

It began with me telling lies about sins I hadn't committed, just to have something to say.

From the darkness of other side of the box, I heard him mumble in Latin before eventually saying, 'Your sins are forgiven. For your penance say three Our Fathers and three Hail Marys.'

I was eight years old, but I was in no doubt that this man had the power from God to absolve me from all my sins. From any bad thoughts or deeds. All I had to do was tell him all about them, in detail, and say I was sorry. Stuff I wouldn't tell my best friend.

I always hated going to confessions, but here I am, back again after forty-seven years, at the end of a queue waiting my turn. Monsignor Malachy Flanagan's name is over the door, but it's not his forgiveness I'm looking for.

~

When I made my first Communion, my mother was too sick to be there. Dad brought me and my three-year-old brother, Dessie, to see her in hospital after the ceremony. She could hardly open her eyes. Dad stood by the window looking down into the car park while Dessie held my hand and stared at the liquid flowing through the tubes and into the glass jar under Mam's bed.

'You look nice,' she whispered, but I don't think she could really see me. She sounded so weak. Taking short sharp breaths with every few words.

'I want you to promise me … that you'll look out for Dessie, Joe.'

I nodded, even though she still couldn't see me.

'I will, Mam.'

'Promise me.'

'I promise.'

That was the last thing she ever said to me.

On the following Sunday, I wore my communion suit to her funeral. I held Dessie's hand at the grave as we watched her coffin being lowered into the ground. The priest said prayers and threw holy water. Then we went home.

~

'What's going to happen to the two lads when their father goes back to the Lebanon?'

'Someone's going to have to look after them.'

Then a silence.

I sat on the stairs and listened as Granny and my old aunts tried to figure out what to do with us. Dessie wanted to come down too, but I told him to stay in his bed.

The priest had his say. He whispered so quietly that I could barely hear him.

'They need a woman to look after them. For a while, anyway.'

Everyone was quiet in the front room.

'Ye will have to share the burden between ye,' the priest said sternly to Granny and my three aunts. 'To help them cope with losing their mother. In a few years, they can go to boarding school, and they'll be well looked after there.'

The four women looked at each other but knew there was no point in arguing. They nodded their heads in reluctant acceptance and continued to sip tea and eat cake.

I made my way quietly upstairs to our room where Dessie was already asleep. I got into bed and lay awake all night, fearful of what the future held for us. Troubled about what had been decided for me.

~

For the next ten years, we were unwelcome guests in our family's homes. Granny hadn't the energy, while my aunts had their own troubles to deal with. At least, that's what they said. We were passed around like unwanted baggage.

Six months after the funeral, my father came home from the Lebanon. We got to stay with him for a couple of weekends. That was all that was allowed. I wanted him to tell us about his job, but he never said very much.

'Dad, when can I join the army? I want to be like you.'

'When you grow up, Joe.'

Before we had time to get to know him again, he was gone. Another tour of duty. He said he had to go, but I knew he didn't. He could have looked for time at home. He didn't want us either.

We were on our own mostly and I took care of Dessie. On school days, I got him out of bed and helped put on his clothes. If we had time, there was food on the table of whatever house were in, but we didn't always have time to eat it. I walked with him to school, and then he had to wait for me to bring him home in the evenings. I was more than just a big brother to him. He looked up to me, and I took care of him. I didn't have time for other friends.

I was twelve when I went to boarding school. The priest and my father had it all planned out. It meant he didn't have to worry about us—if he ever did. I was glad to get away, but worried for little Dessie. He was only seven and had to continue living with Granny or one of the three aunts. In the beginning, I wrote to him every week and I stayed with him during holiday breaks.

After a few years, the letters became less frequent, and I began to stay with friends for holidays. Dessie was very different to me. Quiet and shy. Not much into sport. Liked music. Kept to himself mostly. We were already drifting apart.

~

This queue for confessions is starting to move a bit faster now. There's about five ahead of me. All old women. What could they have done wrong? I'll be in there by ten to three. That should be enough time. The Pope's Mass in the Phoenix Park starts at three and they're showing it on the big screen here in the church. There's a lot of speculation about what he's going to say. Must be three or four hundred people in here. Too old or too sick to get to the Park. Most of them know they haven't long left, and here they are, praying for the salvation of their souls. They're in the right place but at the wrong time. That's something I know all about.

~

'Crawley, you are going to tell me the name of the other boy or you will take the beating for both of you,' Fr Robby roared at me.

It was my second year in the school, and I was in big trouble. I was thirteen and I was scared. A man of God was about to beat the crap out of me for going to the dormitory at lunchtime with another boy. Everyone knew it wasn't allowed, but Johnny Fields and myself needed to get our football gear. We forgot to take it with us that morning.

As we made our way down the backstairs, we heard Fr Robby's door opening. We made a run for it, but I was caught.

'Tell me the boy's name,' the priest roared again. As he tightened his grip on my clothes, I felt my two feet leave the ground. There was rage in his eyes. I saw it as he lifted me higher. I saw his white band of authority shining out from inside the collar of his black flowing cassock. I struggled to free myself. His left hand appeared to my right. There was a flash of light. Something shiny. In his hand. He held it higher so that I could see it clearly. A golf club. An iron. It must have been the easiest thing to grab when he ran from his room. Now it was a weapon. His weapon.

He released his grip and I fell to the floor. As I tried to crawl into the corner of the landing to get away from him, he whacked me across my back and then on my legs. I curled up in a ball of pain. He continued to beat me for what seemed like an eternity.

When he finally stopped, he stood over my shaking body and roared, 'Now get back to your class and never let me catch you on these stairs again.'

That night in bed, I hurt all over. I tried not to move. My arms and legs were badly bruised from the blows of his golf club.

'Fair play to you, Spider, for not grassing on me,' Fields whispered in the dormitory.

It was small consolation as I lay awake in agony for a long time wondering how such a man could call himself a priest. Dress like a priest. Act like a priest. Moralise like a priest. And then beat the crap out of a boy who had been brought up to respect and obey men in his position. Men who had a vocation. A call from God. Or, as I think about it now, maybe he needed to get to a place where he could express his sadistic cravings with the security of a black cassock and white collar to protect him.

There were more like him. Fr Kelvin could barely control himself at the start of his class. He'd pace up and down and glance through the homework of some of the better kids. All nods and smiles until he arrived at the desk of Derry Kirwan. With one hand already on his leather belt, he'd ask Derry for his work.

'Now, Derry, is there any hope that you managed to get your work done for today?'

There was never any hope, and Fr Kelvin would quickly remove his belt from his substantial girt and wallop Derry five times on both hands. It became a ritual. Derry

Kirwan was not a scholar and never would be. No matter how often the priest tried to beat it into him. It was hopeless, but then Fr Kelvin knew that. My eyes squeezed shut, but I couldn't shut it out. With every blow, I felt Derry's pain on my own flesh. But, for the priest, each blow delivered gave him some sort of perverted pleasure.

They wanted me to play on school teams, but I was only interested in looking after myself. I refused. I spent a lot of time in the gym getting strong and fit. My mind was made up. After school, I was going to join the army. I saw the life my father had and decided it was for me. He was doing exactly what he wanted. He didn't give a shit about anyone else and nobody messed with him. I still wrote to Dessie. Saw him during holidays.

~

'Spider', they christened Dessie when he arrived at the school. He wasn't too happy. It was my old nickname. I had left the previous June and he'd inherited it. Not that there was much wrong with 'Spider', and you could understand where it came from with a name like Crawley.

> Dear Dessie,
> I hope you are keeping well as I am myself, thank God.
> Everything is going well with my training. Biggest news is the arrival of women at the camp. Women in Dad's army! He won't be too happy. Did you hear from him?
> Keep writing the letters. And I'll write when I can. How is school?
> JC

I could have written more often, but we were kept very busy in the Curragh and besides, I was never good at writing letters. He wrote to me every couple of weeks in the first few years. After a while, I only heard from him every now and again. I thought he was settling in, making friends. Didn't need me as much.

I was busy doing my own thing. Looking after myself. I was doing well. We were drifting further apart.

That's when I stopped worrying about him. Stopped looking out for him.

~

Fr Malachy Flanagan (or Mal, as he liked to be called) had arrived in the school while I was there. He taught me Latin for a year. Or, at least, he tried to. I had little other contact with him. He didn't take sports, and I wasn't a candidate for the annual musical he produced. Those who were got his full attention and he was more than generous to his leading lads. Trips to the beach at weekends. Trips to Dublin for shows. Late night viewing of films in his room. He was very popular among his troupe. Dessie became part of that.

Was it God that called Mal to the priesthood? To become His servant and spread the gospel. To teach and guide His flock. Or was it someone or something else that steered him? Some deep-rooted instinct that called him to take his holy vows. To put him in a position of authority and trust where he could be among innocent and vulnerable young boys.

Right now, I'm the last one in line for confessions. I'll be in there in a minute. Everyone else in the church is standing up now. Foostering through their leaflets to find the right place. Singing along with all the choirs in the Phoenix Park. 'A Joy for all the Earth' is what they're singing. Specially written for the Pope's visit. He'll be arriving soon to say Mass and give his homily. Bringing joy to all the earth? We'll see about that.

~

'Young Crawley,' the Sergeant would shout at me, 'Show them how it's done.'

And I would take on any challenge they threw at me. They thought I was level-headed and calm in difficult situations, but the truth was, I didn't give a shit. About anyone or anything.

'We're moving you to the ordnance corps,' I was told by the sergeant. 'You're a bollix, but you're a bollix with a cool head.'

The unit was being expanded to cope with all the dissident activity at the time. The IRA had ended their armed campaign in Northern Ireland in 1997, but a few breakaway groups not happy with the ceasefire continued with a low-level campaign. Much of this was coming from south of the border. I was appointed as a technical officer.

It didn't take long before I got to grips with the job, and I was regularly involved in diffusing or disposing of explosives. I got a kick out of blowing stuff up. The kind of stuff that could kill or injure innocent people. It was simple enough. Identify the target and risks. Calculate what's needed to get rid of it. Set the charge and— BANG!—it's gone. Problem eliminated. They liked what I did, and they admired my attitude. I was offered promotion a few times, but I had no interest in managing people or looking after them. I wanted to be in control. I didn't need anyone making decisions for me. I knew what had to be done and just got on with it.

~

I never wanted to get married or have kids, but when Maggie told me she was pregnant, I gave in. We had been seeing each other for a few years, but it was more a physical than emotional thing for me. Her family was very religious, and she didn't want to upset them with the news. So we got married in a hurry. Seven months later, the baby was born. I was delayed getting to the hospital, and when I finally got there, Maggie was inconsolable. There had been talk about the baby's heart being poorly before he was born, but we never expected this.

'I'm sorry to have to tell you that your son has Down's Syndrome,' the doctor said to Maggie. 'Because of your age, Mrs Crawley, the odds were one hundred to one,' he added.

I stood by the window looking down into the car park. *Ninety-nine kids are perfect, and I get the one.*

Maggie got over the initial shock better than I did, and she took good care of Ryan. I never came to terms with it. I couldn't cope with people looking at my kid like that. Knowing there was something wrong with him. Smiling at us. Feeling sorry for him. For us. For me. Like the time my mother died, and my father didn't want us. Their pity sickened me.

~

Any feelings I had for Maggie quickly disappeared. When I was in the house, we were constantly shouting at each other. Fighting over the smallest things. Upsetting the kid, too. I had to get out.

'You can't leave us like this!' Maggie pleaded with me.

'I've had enough. You two will be better off without me,' I said and moved out. I'm not sure what she's up to now. As far as I know she has a council house. I don't see much of them. I live alone and keep to myself.

~

When Dessie heard I was leaving Maggie and the kid, he couldn't understand how I could do that to them. He had been a reluctant best man at my wedding. Mostly, he kept to himself. He sang a few songs in the church. Later that year, he was godfather to Ryan at his christening. He was always better to them than I was. He had a few girlfriends himself down through the years, but they didn't last long, and he never got married. He lived alone and survived on social welfare and the odd job now and again. When Maggie told him the news, he was furious. He tracked me down and tried to get me to change my mind.

'You'll have to look after them,' he pleaded with me.

His outburst took me by surprise. It wasn't like him. He was always the quiet one. He used to look up to me.

'You wouldn't understand,' I said, dismissing him.

'You're selfish and only care about yourself. With all the opportunities you had, you've thrown them all away,' he shouted at me and then left.

I didn't hear from him again until eight months ago when he rang to tell me that our father had died. It came as a bit of a surprise. I knew my father had Alzheimer's for years and that he was in a nursing home in south Dublin, but I never went to see him. I heard it was some sort of fancy place for those who could afford it. Retired army officers, bankers, priests and the like.

This is where Monsignor Malachy Flanagan, or Mal, as we once knew him, came back into our lives. He had risen through the ranks, found favour at home and abroad and was eventually appointed monsignor at the national seminary for priests, with the Pope's approval. Some years after he retired, they closed the place and now send any prospective priests to Rome. He told me all this when I met him at the funeral. He came over to sympathise with me in the small chapel in the nursing home. He said he had become a close friend to my father during his time in the nursing home. Sat with him nearly every day and comforted him as his condition worsened.

'I only wished I could have done more,' he said humbly.

Then, he asked me about Dessie.

~

The coffin was in a small room beside the chapel and it was open. I didn't go in there. I had seen so little of my father in the past, I didn't need to see him dead.

Dessie was in there. Shaking hands with the few

friends who came to pay their respects. I watched from the door as the monsignor made his way in. He stood by the coffin, made the sign of the cross over the body then turned and offered his outstretched hand in sympathy to Dessie.

Dessie was ashen-faced. It was as if he had seen a ghost. He stood there with his mouth open, saying nothing. The monsignor leaned forward and embraced him. There was a look of terror on Dessie's face. He stood motionless as Mal moved away and left the small room, nodding his head as he passed me in the corridor.

Everyone was asked to leave as the lid was placed on the coffin. I asked Dessie if he was all right. He looked at me for a brief moment but said nothing.

In the graveyard, we stood on opposite sides as the coffin was lowered into the ground. The same grave where my mother was buried all those years ago. Maggie stood beside Dessie with the kid. Ryan was nearly a man now. He held onto Dessie's hand as the priest threw holy water onto the coffin. I waited until everyone had left and stood alone by the grave. I had no words to say but kept hearing my mother's voice in my head. Over and over:

'Promise me you'll look out for Dessie, Joe.'

~

A couple of weeks after the funeral, we met to sort out a few things with the solicitor. Dessie didn't look well. I was worried he wasn't taking care of himself. I suggested that I call around to visit him. He didn't answer me. He was in a hurry to get away.

After a couple of days, I tried calling him on his phone but there was no reply. I went to his house and eventually had to break a pane of glass in the kitchen window to get in.

I found him upstairs in the bedroom. He was alive. Just about. He hadn't eaten in days and he was in a mess. I

got him water and food and cleaned him up as best I could.
I put him sitting in his chair. I asked him what was wrong.
When he finally spoke, his voice was only a whisper and,
for a time, almost incoherent.

'Flanagan. Mal,' he said.

'Monsignor Flanagan. In the nursing home? The music
teacher?'

'He destroyed me.'

'How Dessie? How did he destroy you?'

'He told me I was his favourite pupil. His best singer.
He said he was going to take care of me.'

I could see the fear in his eyes. He had never spoken
about Flanagan before or what he did to him. Maybe he
had forgotten about it? Hidden it away somewhere.? Seeing
the man at the funeral brought it all back.

'He raped me.'

I knelt quietly beside Dessie as he struggled to tell me
what happened all those years ago. There were tears
running down his cheeks. I struggled to hold back my own
tears.

'It's all right Dessie,' I said. 'It wasn't your fault.'

I tried to console him. I didn't want to hear any more.

He was shaking all over and started to cough violently.
I stood up and put my arm around his shoulder. His head
went forward suddenly, and he threw up the few bits of
food he had eaten.

'I'll help you, Dessie,' I told him as I tried to clean his
face and clothes with a cloth. 'You need to be strong.
Flanagan will get what's coming to him.'

'It's too late. He's an old man.' He was crying now.

'I'll get you help. Medical help. And counseling.
Whatever it takes. And I'll make sure Flanagan gets what
he deserves, I promise you.'

I got him to drink more water and then left to get food
and fresh clothes for him.

When I got back to his house a couple of hours later, there were three squad cars and an ambulance outside.

What had remained hidden deep inside Dessie had been released and he couldn't cope with it. He shot himself in the head with his shotgun shortly after I left.

~

The door has just opened on the confessional and an old woman is stepping out with her head bent and her rosary beads held tightly in her bony hands. She is already saying her penance.

I step into the box, close the door behind me, then turn around and sit on the small wooden seat. It's like going back in time.

Suddenly the wooden shutter between us is jolted back, and I can just about see him through the metal grill. He's sitting too but stooped over with his head down. I sit in silence looking at him. Thinking about all the vile things he did to Dessie and to so many others. And then he had the gall to sit with my father in his dying days. Inside, I'm burning with rage. The very thought of being in this confined space with him makes me sick to the core. But I have a promise to keep.

He's in a hurry. The Pope's Mass is about to start. He gets impatient.

'May the Lord be in your heart and help you confess your sins with true sorrow,' he whispers.

~

Six months earlier my commanding officer sent me to see the company doctor.

'What for?' I asked him.

'You're not yourself since your brother died. You need help.'

He was right. Dessie's death, the way he died, why he died, changed me. I let him down over the years. I hadn't looked out for him like my mother asked me to on her deathbed. Her last words to me. I spent every minute of every day thinking about that and how I could make amends. At night, Dessie would talk to me. He would stand by my bed and hold my hand. He was lost. Wandering in the darkness. Searching. Things needed to be put right. So that he could find her. Our mother. I promised him I would make it all right.

~

At work, I was anxious. I couldn't keep my mind on the job. I started making mistakes. Dangerous mistakes. Some people got hurt. Not seriously, but enough to get me sent to the doctor. He referred me to the army psychologist. They put me on tablets and encouraged to take time off. I wasn't ready. Not yet.

Then, one day, I read in the paper that the Pope was coming to Ireland in a few months. The article went on to suggest that he should use the visit to apologise on Irish soil for the cover-up by the church of child sex abuse.

I knew my time had come. This was the opportunity I was waiting for. I packed in my job with the army, but before I left I managed to take out a few bits and pieces that would come in handy later on.

~

I found out that Flanagan concelebrated Mass from time to time in the Mountrock Church, close to the nursing home. It wasn't far from where I lived, so I started attending Mass there as soon as I retired. I got my name on a roster for cleaning and helping out with odd jobs.

Everything came together when the parish newsletter announced that Monsignor Flanagan would be hearing confessions on the Sunday of the Pope's Mass, as most of the other priests in the diocese would be in the Park. The older people still preferred a one-on-one in the confessional box. I helped install the big screen and projector and arranged to check it all on the Saturday night, to make sure everything was functioning for the next day's big show. I also checked the live webcam to make sure it was broadcasting and recording from the church.

~

'Listen very carefully to what I have to say, Monsignor Malachy Flanagan. Or would you prefer if I called you Mal?'

Through the grill, I can see the shadow of his old body stiffen in the darkness. He raises his shoulders a little and moves his head closer to the metal grill between us.

'I have planted five kilograms of explosives under the altar and beneath the floorboards in the nave of this church. I am holding the detonator in my hand. It's enough to kill you, me and everyone else here. Do you understand?'

No answer, so I ask again.

'Do you understand what I just said?'

'I understand,' comes the trembling reply. 'But why? Why would you do this? What do you want?

'Do you remember, Dessie—Spider Crawley? Your favourite singer?'

More silence from beyond the grill. The Mass has started, and I can hear the Pope speaking from the Park through the church loudspeakers.

I raise my voice a little more and say, 'This is for Dessie and all the other innocent boys you abused from the sanctuary of your black cassock and white collar. Do you remember them?'

Still nothing.

'You destroyed Dessie's life. He's dead because of what you did to him. You know that.'

'What do you want me to do?'

'I want you to confess your sins. All of them. In detail. And ask for forgiveness.'

'From who?'

'From God, for a start. Do you think He'll forgive you? '

No answer. His head is in his hands.

'Listen to me, Mal. Sit up and listen to me. What you did is unforgivable. So let's try something else. OK?'

'Yes, yes. OK. Whatever you want.'

'You will leave this confessional box and, for your penance, you will walk slowly to the pulpit, take the microphone and say the following.'

'But I can't do that. The Mass. His Holin—'

'Listen carefully, Mal. Do as I say, and we all walk out of here alive. If you don't, everyone dies. Do you get that?'

'Yes, yes, I get that.'

'Good. Get to the altar and take the microphone. Tell the congregation that you are a bad priest. That you sexually abused young boys throughout your ministry. Then apologise for what you did, especially for what you did to Dessie Crawley. Say his name. I want to hear his name.'

He's getting up, slowly. Standing. Still hunched over. His hand is on the door.

'Remember, Mal, my finger is on the detonator. Our lives are in your hands.'

~

I'm staying in here. I can see him through a gap in the purple curtain. He's making his way along the aisle to the altar. No one is passing any heed. The other priest has seen him now. He nods and smiles at him. Hearing confessions is never easy. Everyone is watching the Pope on the big screen. Flanagan's stopped at the altar and is looking back at me. At the confessional box. *Keep going you bastard. Keep going.* He's walking again. To the pulpit. Climbing the steps and taking the mic.

My hand is shaking. My finger hovers over the detonator switch, but it keeps moving, shaking. It never shook before. All those times I had to deal with dangerous situations. They never bothered me. I didn't care. But I care now. I have to do this for Dessie. To help him find our mother. I promised him.

Flanagan's coughing into the microphone. Clearing his throat. Trying to get everyone's attention. The second priest is standing up. Seeing if he's all right. He's put up his hand to stop him, to reassure him. People are looking at him now. Waiting for him to speak.

'My name is Monsignor Malachy Flanagan and I am a bad priest.'

I can feel the tension in the church. *Go on say it. Say all of it.*

'I sexually abused young boys throughout my life as a priest.'

The congregation all gasp at his words. *Apologise.*

'I want to apologise for what I did ...' He's looking down in my direction. 'Especially for what I did to Dessie Crawley.'

That's it. The apology. In front of all these people. He did it.

That's for you Dessie. I'm sorry I let you down in the past. And for you Mum. I did look out for him in the end.

~

There's silence in the church. Everyone is still staring in shock at Flanagan. On the big screen by the altar, there's silence in the Park as the Pope makes his way to the lectern. This is his chance to apologise for the abuse and cover-ups in his church in Ireland. This is his opportunity to respond to the calls from politicians, the press and even from some priests. If he does apologise will it make any real difference? Anywhere? And if he doesn't, then what? Nothing will change. This is my chance to make sure it never happens again. I owe it to Dessie. To all the other kids.

It's simple really. Identify the target and risks. Calculate what's needed to get rid of it. Set the charge and—BANG!—it's gone. Problem eliminated.

The story will make headlines all over the world. The Pope's visit overshadowed by a suicide bombing at a Catholic church. Hundreds dead. They'll soon figure out 'what' happened. Then the 'who' bit? And eventually the 'why?' Flanagan's apology is recorded and accessible on the parish website. That will show the world what kind of a monster he was. And I left a note in my apartment, just in case.

My hand has stopped shaking now. My finger is on the detonator. I press the button. The last thing I hear before the explosion is the voice of His Holiness as he starts his homily:

'*Confiteor Deo omnipotenti, et vobis, fratres ...*'

~

'What did he say?' the army sergeant asked. 'He wasn't making any sense.'

The hospital chaplain stepped away from the bed:

'It was Latin,' he explained. 'He was making a last confession. Saying he was sorry.'

'Unfortunately, he was so badly injured in the explosion at the barracks that there was very little we could do for him,' the doctor added. 'He's been delirious since the ambulance brought him in here.'

'It was going to be his last job,' said the sergeant. 'Simple enough by his standards. Dispose of five kilograms of explosives. Then he was going to retire. It all went desperately wrong.'

Holding on to anger is like grasping a hot coal with the intent of throwing it at someone else; you are the one who gets burned.

~**Buddha**

Let the Punishment Fit the Crime

Alix Moore

Monday, 5 September 1983, 9.00 a.m.
Aldfield Grange Public School for Boys, North Yorkshire

I saunter into the school assembly hall and slide into a row halfway down that is already crammed with my fellow sixth-formers: eighteen-year-old lanky scrotes, redolent of testosterone and fag smoke. Trying not to breathe in too deeply, I elbow my way past these unsavoury sons of peers, politicians and pools-winners and claim my rightful place in the middle of the row.

Crispin Leghorne, current favourite of Mr Finn, the music master, finishes massacring 'Jerusalem' on the piano as our headmaster, Dr Peter 'Scarface' Kennedy, limps into the hall and climbs the five steps onto the stage. Placing his cane on the lectern, he surveys us as we sit in serried ranks on the rows of wooden benches that are crammed into the magnificent, medieval hall. A shaft of sunlight slants in through the high-set, stained glass windows and illuminates his face: a livid patchwork of mottled skin bisected by raised, red ridges of scar tissue; his left eye barely visible, the flesh around it a puckered mess of skin grafts. The new boys in the front row look up at him and shiver with a nascent, superstitious fear. His ruined appearance will be the cause of many nightmares in the junior dormitories, but there is also an element of hero worship amongst them for the man who was a fighter pilot until the day his Hawker Harrier executed a fiery nose dive into the North Sea.

Scarface clears his throat several times and taps his

cane on the lectern. 'Good morning, gentlemen. Today is the first assembly of the new school year, and I would like to welcome our first-formers to Aldfield Grange.' He bestows a ghastly, rictus smile on the pathetic little runts. 'The first day at a new school can be daunting, but I am sure that all of us, teachers and pupils alike, will work together to help you to settle in.' He sweeps his gaze over the rest of us and pauses as he spots me. I lift my chin and maintain eye contact for a few seconds. He is the first to look away, and I realise I have successfully pushed a button as the nervous tic, another souvenir of the plane crash, has him capering like a dancing bear for a few humiliating seconds. A ripple of amusement runs through the hall, and I pretend to cough into my hand whilst hissing, '*Tosser!*'

I tune out as he drones through his valedictory speech and let my eyes feast on the scrumptious Pandora, Scarface's secretary, who is sitting on the stage, legs crossed modestly at the ankle and looking as if butter wouldn't melt. I allow myself the pleasure of remembering the previous afternoon when, no more than an hour after my return from the endless, tedious summer vacation spent in London with the two strangers who are my parents, there had been a gentle knock on the door of my bedroom.

'Come in,' I'd drawled, thinking that if it was that idiot Culpepper trying to persuade me to join the rugby team, I'd show him just how great I am at kicking.

The door opens and Pandora slips into the room, fresh as a daisy in a summer frock and high-heeled sandals. She gives me a slow, sexy smile. 'Hope I'm not disturbing you, Oliver? Just wanted to welcome you back.'

I decide to play it cool. 'Pandora. What a nice surprise. I was only thinking of you last week.'

She pouts. 'I hope your summer was better than mine. Two weeks in Clacton with Fred and the rest of the time spent decorating our bedroom.'

I'm reflecting on how wonderfully common she is when, without warning, she propels herself across the room and latches onto my mouth. I pull away smartly. In my experience, women's mouths are full of lies, eager to betray others' secrets and confidences and, as a consequence, I prefer not to be kissed on the mouth. But I soften my action by caressing her firm, little derrière because I cannot afford to offend Pandora and her easy mouth at the moment. She's too useful to me.

Pandora flounces over to the bed and sits on the edge, her dark eyes narrowed as she studies me closely. 'Is everything alright? You seem different somehow, more … muscular.'

I grin. 'Must be all of the tennis I played.'

'Who with?'

'That would be telling.' I go and sit next to her on the bed and watch as she starts to roll gossamer stockings down her smooth, sun-kissed legs. I put my hand in the small of her back and pull her round so that she is facing me. 'Did you miss me?'

'Yes' she whispers, her pupils so dilated that I can see tiny reflections of myself in them.

'Prove it.' I say.

And she does.

~

The sound of my surname jolts me back to the reality of the assembly hall to find Scarface glaring at me.

I have no idea what he has just said. 'I beg your pardon, headmaster.'

Scarface scowls and says, 'I just asked you whether you would like to share the news of your father's achievement with the school.'

I stare back at him, trying not to betray the fact that I don't know what he is talking about. My father was barely around this summer, choosing instead to boost the family coffers by undertaking as much private work as he could. Whatever he has achieved, he hasn't shared it with me. So I say, 'I would prefer that you tell the news, sir,' and brace myself—the fried eggs I had for breakfast earlier curdling in my stomach.

Scarface says, 'Professor James Worthington, Oliver Worthington's father and an ex-Head Boy of this school, has been awarded a knighthood for his services to medicine. Please join me in applauding his success.'

I sit while they politely clap, noting the smirks and sniggers of my fellow classmates.

When the grudging applause finishes, Piers Pond-Smythe, who is sat next to me, raises his hand. 'What did he do sir? To get the knighthood, I mean.'

'Professor Worthington has developed a device called a grommet which is used to treat children suffering from a condition called serous otitis media, commonly known as "glue ear".'

There is a smattering of laughter at this, and Piers whispers in my ear, 'Hey, Gluey Grommet—bet you're proud of your old man.'

'Silence!' Scarface thunders out, glaring at our row, and I have to bite back my response.

After we have crucified both verses of 'I Vow to Thee, My Country', my form master, Richard Tredmore, walks to the front of the stage. He is immaculately turned out: feet shod in shiny Oxford lace-ups, crisp white shirt and old school tie, and his curly dark hair precision-parted to the left. Tredmore regards us earnestly for a moment. 'The headmaster has asked me to set the school challenge for this term, and I have given it some careful thought over the summer holidays. The school's motto is *Spectemur agendo* which means: let us be judged by our actions. I have therefore decided that your challenge this term is to carry out as many random acts of kindness as you can. In other words, that you should take every opportunity that presents itself to show kindness to others. For example, offer to carry the old lady's shopping bag to the bus; or pay somebody a compliment; or help a classmate with that tricky piece of homework.'

One of the fifth formers in front of me whispers to his neighbour, 'I'm going to offer to warm Pandora's bed for her. That would be the ultimate act of kindness.' I lean forward and viciously twist his ear, enjoying the feeling of gristle and cartilage crunching between my fingers.

Tredmore concludes, '... and remember, gentlemen, any kind action should be undertaken selflessly without expecting any more recompense than a simple "thank you". One of this school's many aims is to produce young men who are kind and compassionate; who genuinely care about others; who are honourable and who possess moral fibre. We all need to work harder to achieve these virtues. Are there any questions?'

He is met with a stony silence, and I idly wonder if I should ask him whether buggering second formers would count as an act of kindness. If his answer is in the affirmative, a number of the teachers and prefects will win the challenge hands down. Instead, I assume an eager expression and shoot my hand into the air.

Tredmore smiles at me. 'Yes, Worthington.'

'Please, sir, when can we start? I can't wait to undertake my first random act of kindness for somebody in need.'

A collective groan sweeps the hall accompanied by the sounds of boys pretending to retch.

'Silence!' thunders Scarface, resuming command. 'The challenge starts today. You will be asked to prepare an essay at the end of term detailing your actions and what you have learned from them.'

There is a general shuffling of feet as two hundred

boys gather satchels and sporting paraphernalia and prepare to leave the hall.

Scarface taps the lectern with his cane. 'Not so fast, gentlemen. Before you depart for your lessons, I need to invite Hewitt Major onto the platform for "six of the best" following his appalling insolence in class yesterday.'

'Does that count as an act of kindness, sir?' calls a wag from the back who is also hauled onto the stage for his trouble. As Scarface expertly wields his cane, I shut my eyes and imagine the ultimate act of kindness: ridding the school of Scarface.

~

Three days later a wide-eyed first-former comes to my room as I am getting ready to go down for lunch and whispers, 'The headmaster wants to see you in his study.'

I give him a smart clip round the ear for his trouble and make my way to Scarface's office. I don't bother knocking on the door and saunter in, pausing a moment to admire the sight of Pandora bending over to put a file in the bottom drawer of a grey metal cabinet.

I say quietly, 'Why does he want to see me?'

Pandora whips round at the sound of my voice and goes scarlet. 'Good grief, Oliver, I didn't hear you come in.'

'You know I like to keep you on your toes, unlike that wet lettuce of a husband of yours.'

'SShhh ...'

I raise my voice a tad. 'What are you worrying about? Scarface isn't going to hear us through the door, not with those melted stumps for ears.'

Pandora looks terrified. She depends on this job to supplement the paltry wage her husband brings home from his job as a postman. She whispers, 'He thinks that you are responsible for the "glue incident".'

I shrug. 'And what do you think, Pan?'

She refuses to meet my eye and mutters, 'I just hope it wasn't anything to do with you, Oliver. Piers is still in hospital and can't hear a thing. The glue penetrated his eardrum.'

I briefly relish the memory of sneaking into Pier's room the night before last and putting a few drops of superglue into his ear while he was sleeping. Let the punishment fit the crime. I assume a concerned expression. 'Oh dear, maybe my father could take a look at him.'

Pandora gives me a sharp look. 'You'd better go through. He won't tolerate lateness.'

~

Scarface is sitting at his desk writing on a notepad. As I walk into his office he looks up and then continues writing. I know that it is a ploy to discomfort me, and I take the opportunity to have a look round the room. Pandora told me that she once walked in and saw him cleaning a gun, which he explained was his service revolver. I would give anything to get my hands on that and report him to the police. Every spare space is crammed with dusty books and papers, but my eye is caught by a framed photograph that is displayed on top of the bookcase nearest to me. It is of a younger, unscarred Scarface sitting next to a pretty, dark-haired woman who is holding a little girl in her lap. The woman and Scarface look slightly startled, as if the photographer caught them unawares, but the little girl is grinning from ear to ear. I find myself unusually intrigued. This is a side of Scarface that I didn't know about, and I make a mental note to ask Pandora about it the next time I plumb her velvety depths.

Scarface throws down his pen and sighs. 'So, Worthington, what do you have to say for yourself?'

'About what?'

'About what, sir,' he barks.

'About what, *sir*,' I repeat, injecting the merest hint of

insolence into my tone.

He gets up and walks round to the other side of the desk, perching on the edge of it, his gown hanging loose. Up this close, his face looks like a plastic carton that has been too near the fire.

'About the fact that some time on Tuesday night you dropped glue into Pond-Smythe's right ear.'

'Sorry, sir. I don't recall doing that.' I stare back at him unblinkingly and watch a vein throb in his left temple; delight in seeing him struggle to control the tic in his eyelids; hope he's going to lose it completely. I'm not disappointed.

Scarface grabs a cane that is lying on his desk and brings it down on my left shoulder. I instinctively put my hand up to protect myself, and he whips the cane across my fingers twice, hard. I look into his face and see spittle frothing in the corner of his mouth, smell rank sweat as he raises the cane above his head, see the fury in his eyes as I grab at the cane and manage to catch it before it lands. As we are grappling to get control of the cane, our hands hampered by the heavy folds of his gown, I hear the door open behind me and a voice say, 'Headmaster!' I immediately let go of the cane and slump into one of the chairs in front of the desk.

Tredmore strides into the room and hurries over to me. 'Are you all right, Oliver?' I nod my head. 'Would you please wait in the outer office? I'll be out in a minute.'

I walk slowly to the door, nursing my injured shoulder. Just before leaving I turn and say, 'I would like to telephone my father, please, sir.'

Tredmore says, 'We can discuss that in a moment. I just need to speak to Dr Kennedy. Shut the door behind you, please.'

As I open the door, Pandora nearly falls into Scarface's office. She's obviously been earwigging. As soon as I have shut the door, she tries to put her arms around me. 'Are you all right? I heard what happened.'

I look at her seriously and say, 'That's good. You can be my witness. The man should be strung up.'

Pandora looks at the floor and mumbles, 'Well, obviously I couldn't hear *everything*, so ...'

I push her away and put my ear to the door.

Scarface is ranting on at Tredmore. He uses words like 'temerity' and 'insubordination' and I can hear the panic in his voice.

Tredmore says, 'We agreed that we would speak to Worthington together. There is no real proof that he was the culprit and—'

Scarface laughs hysterically. 'What proof do you need, Tredmore? You were the one who picked up that the boys were calling Worthington "Gluey Grommet", some of them to his face. You know his history. He's a mental case, a violent yob. I won't tolerate—'

'Headmaster!' It is the first time I've ever heard Tredmore raise his voice. I've always thought he was a bit of a wet.

'How bloody dare you raise your voice to me.' Scarface sounds hysterical, his voice cracked and high.

'I beg your pardon, but I will not stand by and tolerate your unprofessional and, frankly, aggressive behaviour.'

There is a pause, and I wish I could be a fly on the wall, see Scarface's expression. When Tredmore starts to speak again his voice is much quieter, and I can't hear him properly. I take a risk and very gently turn the door handle, pulling against the door to prevent it suddenly opening, carefully inching it open a crack when I feel it unlatch. I look over at Pandora who is sitting behind her desk, hands over her mouth, and put my finger to my lips.

Tredmore continues, 'I told you some months ago that I was unhappy with the level of corporal punishment used in the school. Do we really want this generation to grow up with it, to think it is acceptable and probably go on to treat their own children in the same way?'

Scarface retorts, 'The parents expect us to discipline the boys. Otherwise, they'll never be able to cope with the outside world.'

'There are ways of instilling discipline other than beating and bullying. Let me make myself clear, headmaster. If this continues, I will have no option other than to take the matter to the school governors.'

'That's enough. Get out of my sight!'

'Very well, headmaster, but I am not dropping this.'

I latch the door, scramble to the chair in the corner of Pandora's office and sit in it, covering my eyes with my hand.

I hear Tredmore come out of the office and feel his hand on my shoulder. 'Come along Oliver. Let's go to my office and have a chat. Pandora, could you bring us a pot of tea please?'

~

Tredmore takes a sip of tea and says, 'Did you do it, Oliver?'

I look him in the eye. 'No, sir. My father has spent his life trying to help people with hearing difficulties. Do you honestly think I could do something so terrible, something that would make my father ashamed of me?'

Tredmore holds my gaze for a long moment. 'No, I don't believe you could.'

'Thank you, sir.'

'When I first came to the school—fifteen years ago now—your father was on the Board of Governors. I met him several times.'

I try to look interested. 'Really, sir?'

'Yes. He struck me as a good man. Dedicated to the work that he was doing and genuinely interested in moving the school forward. I remember him being vociferous in his dislike of the use of corporal punishment in any form.'

I nod. 'Father has never laid a finger on me in anger.'

Tredmore stands and goes and looks out of the window. Keeping his back to me he says, 'Of course, you must do what you think is best, Oliver. But I would urge you to continue at the school. You will take your A levels later this year, and I believe you will do well. Starting at a new school at this stage is likely to set you back and that would be a great pity.'

~

Later that afternoon, I stroll back to school having walked into the village to buy some fags and to have a brief debrief session in Pandora's cottage before her husband returns from work. She is still very worked up about what happened this morning and has told me that Scarface has set up a meeting with Tredmore first thing tomorrow morning.

I have decided not to tell my father what has happened with Scarface. Tredmore's words have stayed with me, and I am surprised to feel a grudging respect for the man, despite the fact that he admires my father. Besides, I need to remain at school so I can find a way of exacting revenge on Scarface. If it's the last thing I do, I will make him pay for the beating he gave me earlier.

As I reach the driveway leading down to the school, I am so deep in thought that I nearly knock over a young woman.

'Gosh, I do beg your pardon,' I exclaim.

She steps back. 'No, no, it was as much my fault as yours, I should have been looking where I was going but I was admiring the view over the moors.'

I give her my practised lazy smile and open my eyes wide so that she gets the full benefit of their azure depths. 'Not as lovely as the view I'm admiring, if you don't mind me saying.' I want to punch my fist in the air as I see her pupils dilate and a rosy flush of colour tint her cheeks. Bingo! She's interested. I thank my lucky stars that I dressed in civvies for my stroll. I rapidly consider my next move. She's carrying a suitcase and I say, 'Are you heading for the station? May I carry your case for you?'

She smiles again. 'That's kind of you, but I'm not going to the station, just dropping my luggage off in the gatehouse. I'm staying with my father for a few days. He's the headmaster here.'

It takes every ounce of control I have not to recoil in horror. How on earth can this gorgeous creature be Scarface Kennedy's daughter? She is tall and slim with long dark hair, large grey eyes and a soft, kissable mouth that is curved in the sweetest of smiles. I can see nothing of Scarface in her at all, but, I can now see a strong likeness to the woman I saw in the photograph in his study who must be her mother.

She holds out her hand. 'Sorry, I should introduce myself properly. Diana Kennedy. How do you do.'

I take her soft, cool hand and carefully shake it. 'How do you do.' Her grip is firm, and I find that I don't want to let go. My mind is racing, turning over the possibilities, the delicious potential of this encounter. I certainly don't want to reveal that I am a pupil at the school. 'I'm … I'm Richard Tredmore … I work at the school.' The lie drops easily from my lips.

'Are you a teacher?' She sounds surprised and looks at me intently, probably trying to decide my age.

'I'm a student teacher. I'm here for my practical classroom experience.' I mentally pat myself on the back, pleased at how plausible I sound. We reach the front door of the gatehouse and she pulls a key out of her pocket. If I'm not quick, she'll be gone. I take a deep breath. 'I hope you don't mind me asking, but will you be spending this evening with your father?'

'No. He's supervising sixth-form prep. It's such a lovely evening, I'll probably go for a drive somewhere.'

I lean back against the wall. 'Fancy some company?'

She hesitates for a moment and then nods. 'Give me an hour to unpack and have a bath. Meet you back here at sevenish?'

'It's a date,' I say and hurry off down the drive pondering on how to exploit this golden apple that has unexpectedly landed in my lap.

~

Four hours later I'm lying in bed with Diana in a cosy room tucked into the eaves of The King's Head pub. It's a good way from Aldfield and, fortunately, I haven't seen anybody that I know all evening.

Diana runs a hand down my chest, her fingers cool and fragrant and I feel myself harden in anticipation of a repeat performance. She seems completely comfortable in her skin and devoid of any of the coyness that I have come across in many of the other girls I have slept with. I think it must be that she, like Pandora, is a woman rather than a girl, and I resolve not to bother with girls in the future. And then she goes and spoils it all by trying to kiss me on the mouth, so I flip her onto her back and pin her to the bed.

'Richard, you're hurting my wrists,' she gasps.

'Sorry.' As I thrust into her I think about how easy it is to hurt women: they have such delicate bodies, such fragile egos. When I've finished with her, Diana goes into the bathroom and I roll out of bed, pull on my clothes and run to catch the last bus back to Aldfield.

~

The following morning, I go down to breakfast an hour earlier than usual by way of Scarface's office. The coast is clear at this hour of the morning as Pandora won't arrive for at least another half an hour. I push the envelope under the door. With any luck Scarface will have time to read it before he meets Tredmore. I was up half the night writing it and the words are engraved on my heart:

Dear Dr Kennedy,

I wish to put in writing how deeply concerned I was about the way you treated Oliver Worthington yesterday and your response to my intervention.

Yesterday evening, I felt the need to get away from the school for a few hours to think about how best to deal with the matter and went to The King's Head at Bishop Thornton for a quiet drink.

There was a young woman sitting in the corner of the bar and we started to talk. She was extremely pleasant company and at the end of the evening she told me she had a room upstairs and invited me to join her for a cup of coffee before I went home. I am ashamed to say that I ended up staying the night with her.

The next morning, she asked if she could give me a lift anywhere and I told her that I needed to get back to Aldfield Grange School. She became extremely agitated at this point and eventually confessed that she was your daughter. She had told me her name was Diana but hadn't mentioned her surname.

It would be most unfortunate if this episode became public knowledge, and I believe that the best course of action for all concerned would be for you to resign your post as headmaster of Aldfield Grange. This would also mean that I would not need to report your abusive treatment of pupils to the Board of Governors. I look forward to discussing this with you this morning.

Yours faithfully,

Richard Tredmore

I wipe tears of laughter from my eyes as I imagine Scarface reading it and the discussion that he and Tredmore will have when they meet later this morning.

~

I lie back on snowy pillows and hold Pandora in my arms. When I arrived at her cottage just after lunch, she was in a right old state, sobbing and spluttering. When I enquired what was wrong, she just kept shaking her head and saying, 'I'm not allowed to say. I'm not allowed to say.' She was so near to hysteria that I briskly slapped her face and whisked her into bed for a good seeing to which always seems to have a relaxing effect on her.

Now she has calmed down a bit, I suggest she tells me what has happened. I know it must be something pretty dramatic because we have been given the day off lessons and told to stay within the school boundaries and the place is crawling with police.

She gulps unattractively. 'It was awful. Dr Kennedy asked me to ring the gatehouse so he could have a word with his daughter, Diana, who's staying with him for a few days. I was quite surprised because he hadn't said anything about her coming. So, I got her on the line and put her through to the headmaster and …' Pandora hesitates for a second, a strange expression on her face, '… well, to be honest, I listened in to their conversation for a minute and you'll never guess!'

'What Pandora?

'Dr Kennedy asked Diana where she had been the previous night and she got really shirty with him, saying she was twenty-six years old and wouldn't be treated like a child. And then …' Pandora lowers her voice dramatically, '… he asked her whether she had spent the night with Richard Tredmore.'

'And?'

'She said she had and told him it was none of his

business. He went berserk and started to shout at her. I could hear him from the next room and put the telephone down, which was just as well because Mr Tredmore came in at that point. I could hardly look at him.' Pandora looks at me, eyes wide and full of self-importance.

I grit my teeth and say, 'Come on then, cut to the chase. They haven't closed the school for the day because Tredmore played away with Scarface's daughter!'

Pandora starts to cry again, and I sigh impatiently and try to resist the urge to give her a good slapping. Her eyes have gone slitty with all of the crying and her hair is slightly greasy and smells of last night's dinner. I resolve to bin her after this and idly wonder whether to have a go with the new French mistress who I have only seen from a distance thus far.

Pandora sighs. 'Dr Kennedy came out of his office then and asked me to go and find something in the archive files in the basement. I was only gone fifteen minutes, but when I got back it was all quiet and …' Pandora starts to tremble violently.

'What!' I snap impatiently.

She whispers, 'I knocked on Dr. Kennedy's door and … nothing. So, I went in, and that's when I saw the blood.' Pandora's face pales at the memory and she grabs my hand tightly. 'It. Was. Everywhere.'

I say, 'Gosh, I hope nobody got badly hurt,' and try not to piss myself laughing.

'Hurt?' Pandora is extracting maximum drama from this now and watching the effect of her words on me from under her lashes. 'They were both dead, Oliver. Mr Tredmore was lying face down on the floor with a dirty great hole in his back and Dr Kennedy was slumped over his desk and … part of his head was gone.'

'Gone? What do you mean?'

'He'd been shot in the head. They'd both been shot,

and by the looks of things it was Dr Kennedy who did the shooting. That gun of his was lying on the desk.' Pandora thrusts her head into the crook of my neck and snuffles.

I lie on my back and look up the cracked, yellowing plaster on the ceiling. It couldn't look more beautiful at this moment if Michelangelo himself had painted his best ever fresco on it.

I light a fag and blow out three perfect smoke rings. At this moment, my only regret is that I will never be able to include this particular act of kindness in my end-of-term essay. Let the punishment fit the crime.

Itch

Susan Rodgers

In the end it was not poetic. It was stunning nonetheless. She dipped her finger into the liquid beautiful and traced a design, chunky and rough. Her canvas of skin, coarse, short hair and fabric gave texture to the shape. The only movement he could make was the sluggish blink of grey eyes and the slow rough breath passing through tongue and teeth for the last time. The word that formed within that exhale could only be discerned by one who had lived decades beside him and perhaps his eyes held just enough expression to translate what lips could no longer shape. Why?

She rubbed the blood between two fingers, its consistency already becoming tacky with exposure to the air. She marvelled at the vibrancy of the colour and the quality of its rich viscous feel. It was like no paint or ink she had ever used. In all her imaginings, and there had been many, she had never thought it would be that one instance of rage that would complete the inevitable.

He had come in while she was working. It was late, and she was in a burst of creativity, working furiously to finish up a frame so perfect she felt smug. He had barely realised that she was back working on her art after all these years. He was so caught up in the drivel of modern entertainment on the television, people showing off mediocre talent or knowledge and making fools of themselves every evening, that he never knew she was drawing and getting paid to create illustrations for books that were inferior to her art.

That night he interrupted her. It was earlier than he

usually went to bed. Tap, tap, tap on the door frame to their son, Sean's, old room. His silhouette framed the doorway, no angles, just the rounded lines of his middle-age self. He stood scratching his wrist, peering over his glasses and killing her inspiration.

'What are you working on? Is this your new little hobby?'

She smouldered, trying to pat down the embers of her rage as she reminded him that she had been in touch with an old friend from art school who now headed up the creative department of the children's books branch of a publishing house in London. She was freelancing on a few projects. So, no, it was *not* a hobby, as she was getting paid.

Ernest looked hurt and petulant, but she was beyond remorse.

'That is not fair! It was not my fault that the company needed to cut from the top. They now have someone in half my age and are paying them half of what they paid me.'

'I didn't mean it that way. I'm sorry, Ernest. I just thought it is about time I started using some of my talent and get back in the workforce. I've been home long enough.'

She thought they had traversed the delicate landscape of her resentment. But then he had to open his mouth, letting his words tear open the bindings that kept her anger sealed within.

'Yes, of course, dear. Well, would you like me to help? I can give you my opinions on your doodles and the colours.'

Sound became difficult to define. There was a buzzing in her ears and a pounding in her chest. Her eyebrows felt like the muscles in her forehead had been electrocuted with their involuntary jumping. She was sure his words were poisoning her blood, her brain. She smiled a mouthful of venom that Ernest assumed was real. No, thank you, but she does not need his help. In fact, she is quite tired and will go to bed as well.

She followed his trudge of steps to the landing where the stairs meet the gallery overlooking their small lounge. Their cottage was too small to contain an entire second floor. The complicated ways in which she envisioned Ernest's demise were captured in a tidal wave of raging energy as she stared at his pathetic back. She was overwhelmed by its force and the hate directed at him. With a deep inhale, and before her body has told her head what its intentions are, she heaved forward and pushed him right between the curve of his lower spine and the indistinguishable edges of his lower shoulder blades.

He heaved forward with the force and turned his head in surprise and the improbability of such mutiny. In this way, he did not see his fate, which was a good thing, as he crashed downward and over the barrier of the stairs' railings. A few spindles screaked and splintered as gravity continued to take him at speed to the hard tile floor below him. The thunk of his shoulder and then neck and head impacting the floor was sharp and hard, while the rest of his body was tempered by his clothes and the insulation of his middle-age softness.

She looked down at Ernest arranged on the floor like a Cubist painting: strong angles and lines not quite in the right places. She took a moment to appreciate the image. She tried to analyse how she felt about the scene and searched for repentance—or even sorrow—in the fabric of her emotions but only found a patchwork of relief.

And as she knelt beside Ernest on the floor, she told him why. She was the talented one and he had suppressed her creativity for too long. She had been boxed into a life that was not fitting with her gift. And for this, her creativity and their marriage could not coexist. There never was any other way.

Eventually, she thought he passed. She was not sure, but he was no longer breathing. She went to bed. In the morning she called the Gardaí. Upon hanging up the phone, she went back to the body, bent down, reluctantly wiped away the blood design and hugged him to give the appearance of a devastation she did not feel. The Gardai arrived. She said she woke up and found him there. When questioned she told them she went to bed early and put her earplugs in as the noise of the television sometimes kept her awake. She did not hear a thing. When she got up in the morning, there he was, her beloved. She was distraught, picked him up in her arms and wept.

She asked if anyone wanted tea. She was parched with the effort of going through the emotions she did not feel. Her gaze kept lifting to the ceiling. The guards, an older man and a young woman, thought she was praying to God. Really, she was looking up at her makeshift studio calculating the time it would take to get rid of the body, these people, these distractions and get back to work.

They were too average to be considered a case of foul play. They did not have enough close friends to share their confidences and express any displeasure with their marriage. There were no lovers waiting in the wings on either side. It was an open-and-shut case. In the end, the local newspaper called it an accidental death. The death certificate stated cause of death was injuries sustained in a fall from the stairs. Her son came home from Australia briefly and left soon after the funeral. The neighbours offered condolences and whispered behind her back. They had never liked the way she thought she was better than them and had no interest in having a chat at their local pub. She spent far too much time on her own and the postman delivered packages from Amazon and some publishing house in London. They were sceptical of this behaviour and activity. Her relations with her husband were never in question. There were plenty of women who didn't like their husband. Disliking one's husband did not make the villagers suspicious that she had killed Ernest. They simply did not like her: a blow-in from Dublin.

~

She spends five years doing her penance by enduring the myopia of the small Wexford village. She keeps to herself, lives in her illustrations. She draws constantly. She continues to get more work and children's authors are now requesting her for their books.

Then the time comes when she is ready to shed the skin of the grieving widow, abandoned mother and social outcast. She makes plans and boards the plane.

~

The car is old and not entirely clean. She is not even sure it will make the trip from Athens airport to the holiday cottage on the west coast. It is a three-hour journey, and she is pleased for the language barrier separating herself and the middle-aged Greek man driving. She tries to make herself comfortable in the back seat. He smells in equal parts of garlic and old body odour—wholly, quite repulsive. She knows she should be in the moment and appreciate every nuance of her new environment. But as the landscapes move by her in a stream of colours and shapes, strange Greek sounds play on the radio and the wooden beads swing from the rear-view mirror, she only vaguely registers them, as the images in her head occupy her attention.

There is a happiness she has not felt in many years surrounding her. It is like a protective veneer, not allowing the dirt, smell and disappointing scenery upset her. All these years, and she is finally in Greece on a working sabbatical. An involuntary smile inhabits her lips. The muscles, unused to holding her mouth in this position, tire easily, and it falls from her face. But the excitement is still there. She has succeeded despite everything.

The car slows down as they enter the small village outside Patras. It is October, and while it is much warmer than Ireland, the summer sun has also passed the skies leaving its darker, cooler autumn cousin. The driver stops outside a small house. It is not cute enough to be considered the beachside cottage she booked online, but there is a vague similarity. It looks efficient, so she does not let the disappointment of its façade dampen her spirits. The driver grunts her luggage out of the boot, and it is hastily dumped by the front door. She climbs out of the back seat to join it. She paid for everything online and she is not sure if she should tip or not. The man is hurrying back to his car without any acknowledgement. When she calls, 'Excuse me!' to hand him ten euro, he has already slammed his door and sped off without a backward glance.

She turns to focus on the wood of the sun-bleached front door. As she raises her hand to knock, it opens.

'Hello! You must be Mrs Molloy. Welcome to Greece!'

He offers her his right hand and, once she accepts, his left hand joins it. He is in his mid-thirties. Smooth olive skin, shiny short black hair and professional clothes make her think he is probably the slick real estate agent handling all the online bookings in the area. Bouncing off his leather dress shoes, he shows her around the cottage, giving her tips on starting the hob and how to turn on the shower. She can't tell if he is in a hurry or just energetic. It is a small space, and he walks and talks quickly, so the tour lasts five minutes.

'There is a local lady from our village who will come and clean twice a week and change the linens on the bed,' he tells her as he stands at the front door poised to catapult out.

'Oh no, I don't need anyone to come by. I can take

care of that myself,' she rushes to tell him. She does not want anyone disturbing her creative efforts. She had spent weeks meticulously planning this sabbatical, wanting nothing more than to remove herself from the curious stares and whispered comments that still trail her on trips around the village in Wexford. Even after five years, the rumours follow her like a shadow on a hot summer day: exaggerated, large and never unattached.

'I am sorry, but it is in the contract. The washing machine is very small, and it cannot take the sheets or towels. Just twice a week; you won't even know that she is there.'

Her lips purse wanting to argue but no words come out, only a slight pull of her mouth and a nod to acknowledge it will happen even if she does not wish it.

Once he has left, she sets up her drawing station on the Ikea kitchen table. Her beautiful Japanese brush pens, a gift to herself when she landed her first paid freelance project, were the first items to come out on the table. Slowly she takes out drawing paper and the text she is illustrating. Her hands fondle the paper, delighting in its feel, blankness and boundless possibilities.

The items take up half of the table. She will create an imaginary line and delegate this as her workspace and the other half, her eating space. Only once she is satisfied with the placement of her precious project does she bring her bag into the bedroom and unpack her limited belongings. She sits on the bed and revels in her new-found happiness.

There is a little container of milk in the fridge along with some soft Greek cheese, heavy bread, yoghurt and eggs. She has brought her own tea bags in a Ziploc and decides she will make some tea and go to bed early. The long day of airports, flights, drives and moving into her temporary home have made her exhausted. She will have her tea and go to bed early. Tomorrow she will explore her surroundings, get herself settled and begin to draw.

When she collapses into the bed an hour later, she is too tired to get cross with the lumpy mattress and the damp pillow with its hints of sickly sweet mildew. Her sleep carries her to that deep dream space that only exhaustion can bring.

In her dream, she and Ernest walk down a footpath. The buildings on either side of them are from various stages of their lives. At first, they are outside the art building at college; then the city block outside the advertising agency they both worked for and, finally, the kitchen where they spent so many of their later years in silence. She and Ernest seem so real. The environment around them is not. It is like a two-dimensional space and, while the places are readily recognisable, they look like one of her illustrations.

In the dream, Ernest keeps scratching the eczema on the inside of his wrist, looking around at their surroundings and saying to her, 'But, Marion, real life is better than art.' He keeps repeating it, and she gets angrier each time. She tries to argue that *nothing* is more important, *nothing* is better than good art. Ernest does not seem to hear her. He nods and scratches and continues to look around their caricature background, unimpressed. The more he ignores her, the more enraged she becomes. She wakes in a sweat, disoriented with her surroundings, which are draped in the greys of night and not the technicolour of her dream.

In the morning light, she gets started on her new life. In art school, she had never considered her funny cartoonish characters as art. They were only a means to relieve energy when she was bored. Her doodles are now her bread and butter.

It turns out that doodles are now called illustrations and, with the burgeoning picture-book market for young children, her skill set is in high demand. Six years since her old friend, Sonia, first made contact and she embraced the opportunity. Her life is finally at a place where she can choose her work instead of being assigned projects she doesn't feel highlight her gift.

As she sits in the chair of the designated work space and quickly reviews the story and then her sketchbook with its variations of characters, she works through how she is going to depict the funny little tale about a girl and her brother using their imagination to have exotic adventures in their back garden. She finds the theme tired but is determined to make the images lasting. The author, a famous children's writer, had specifically said she wanted Marion for this new series. The publishing house was very generous with her upfront payments, which afforded her the three months in Greece to complete the project. She had already shown them a few sketches of the general theme of the drawings, and they were positive to the point of ingratiating. She almost felt haughty.

The next few days establish a pattern for her day. She rises when her body tells her and starts the day with a very strong cup of coffee. It is instant coffee, but she overlooks that fact by adding a second spoonful of the granules. She showers and has a light breakfast. Once she fires up her laptop, she sifts through her emails, erasing the advertisements for supplements or exotic holidays and replying to any messages from the publishing house or editors. There are no messages from friends or from her son. It has been a while since she got one of those. There is a vague sensation of loneliness that sits in the pit of her stomach. She fills it with art.

She spends a few hours working on the finishing touches of previous drawings. After noon she goes to the village for lunch and to pick up a few items for supper and her breakfast the following day. Once she arrives back at her cottage, she works on the new drawings and she loses herself in the images until darkness falls. She winds down with a very large glass of the local white wine, which is dry and minerally. Supper is usually a spinach pastry, called spanakopita, from the bakery. She reads a few pages of her book and gets ready for bed. Her routine has been the same for the last few years, ever since Ernest died.

On the Wednesday, the promised housekeeper arrives. A sturdy Greek woman, who looks about her own age, walks through the front door without knocking, carrying a change of sheets and towels. Marion can see by her bucket and limited cleaning supplies that she is also supposed to do some housekeeping in the small cottage. She offers her name quickly as Agda, Agata, or something similar and, in response, Marion says, 'Marion'. It is obvious that neither is looking for camaraderie so there is no need to clarify her name. Marion refers to her as Agnes in her head.

The only thing Agnes seems to dislike more than Marion is cleaning. In reality, she just transfers dust from one spot to another with a cloth that does not qualify as clean to start with and a broom that sweeps back and forth without a dustpan to gather its accumulation. A new routine is established on Wednesday and Saturday mornings. Agnes arrives, and Marion tries to ignore her, with less success than the cleaning woman has slighting her. By the second week, the mutual snubbing becomes too much for Marion. Agnes seemed to mutter to herself in Greek all the time. Marion starts muttering back at her in English and pretends they are having a fulfilling conversation. She hasn't had one of those in a while.

'I am not sure how to take my success as an illustrator. I always imagined that I would be at gallery openings in international cities to rave critical acclaim, not drawing cartoon characters for infants.'

Agnes continues to mumble to herself as if Marion had not said a word.

'Art is still art; Picasso said the important thing is to create.'

Agnes goes about her duties and Marion continues to colour in her sketches. The door is slammed shut when Agnes has deemed her allocated time pretending to clean has been reached. There is no goodbye.

~

After the third week, it starts. She comes home from her walk down to the village and thinks maybe she was stung by an insect or some type of Greek nettle. It is only a small niggle or tingling—an itch—on the inside of her wrist at first. When Agnes arrives the next day, she sits at her table and starts in on her soliloquy to distract her from her niggle. Her voice is faint, not much above a whisper. This way it can be misconstrued as talking to herself—not unusual for an artistic character.

'You know, I have been a widow for five years now. It feels like yesterday and, at other times, a lifetime ago that I had a husband. And even longer since my son was a child.'

Agnes does not break from her low grumbling. That is when Marion notices for the first time that the woman is not talking to herself but has an earbud in one ear with a wire trailing down to the pocket in her housecoat. Marion realises that Agnes must be complaining to the person on the other end of the call.

Marion continues to speak a little louder. 'When we first met, I truly fancied myself in love with him—Ernest, my husband. It's only later that I realised my infatuation was with the life we had dreamed up for ourselves as young idealists. Once he died, I understood what I wanted would never be attainable. I was too old to conquer the world. Nobody took me seriously. But now, look at me! Finally, I am getting to do what I always wanted. I can spend my days drawing.'

Agnes walks out of the room and into the bedroom

with the sheets and towels in Marigold-gloved hands. Marion really doesn't know why her linen needs to be cleaned so often.

She supposes she will pack up and go down to the village for lunch once Agnes leaves. She used to feel awkward about dining alone, attending the theatre or even heading up to Dublin to see a travelling exhibition of an artist that she liked. She hated the looks of pity she would get from the coat attendant. But the worst? It was the women her own age. They would make sure to seat themselves between Marion and their husbands, giving her the side-eye with looks of warning as if she wanted to steal their husband away from them during the intermission of the play. Really! She didn't know how to convey that she had no intention of seducing their husbands. It would ruin the second act for her.

Agnes comes out of the bedroom with sheets and towels balled up and held to her chest. She peers over her wad of cloth, as if hoping Marion has disappeared. Marion starts putting caps on her illustration brushes as she remembers the first months of being a widow.

It was the older men she hated. They were the worst. They kept trying to help her when she didn't need it. She was quite capable and enjoyed her independence after all those years of being trapped in the vacillation of making joint decisions. She wasn't hopeless or desperate. It was all she could do to keep from telling them to bugger off. She wasn't fooled by their chivalry. She had no intention of acquiring a male companion. He would just get in the way.

When she looks up, Marion realises that Agnes has departed and, while she was there, she experienced a slight reprieve from the itch. Now it is back.

The next day she is driven demented. Her brush strokes don't have the refined fine lines she wants. Instead, it is a heavier darker image. She gives up and makes her daily trip to the village. It gets her blood circulating and ensures she eats one hot meal a day.

There are only two cafés open for lunch this time of year. One serves hearty Greek meat dishes and the other seafood. She only eats moussaka at one and squid at the other. She usually takes turns visiting them for lunch, but she is distracted by her skin irritation and can't remember what or where she ate yesterday.

The two attendants lounge outside their respective establishments. When they see her, arms raise and hands start to gesticulate. Like puppets coming to life, they straighten their posture, no longer needing a door frame to hold them up. They pace toward her, arms and mouths moving rapidly as she slowly walks down the road. She favours the side that is home to the moussaka café.

'Madame, would you like traditional Greek food today? The best?'

'Our seafood, very fresh. Just in from the boat.'

As she starts to walk into the moussaka café, the competition walks to the invisible line in the middle of the road in a last-ditch effort to tempt her.

'Ah, beautiful madame, please, you look at the menu?'

'No. Thank you.'

Once she walks through the entrance, the seafood frontman gives up and walks back to his previous spot, settling against the door frame. He looks out toward the pier where the fishermen come in with their catch every day, supplying his restaurant with the tasty squid she will enjoy tomorrow.

With a grand gesture, the moussaka man ushers her in to her chosen café as if she is part of a tourist herd instead of a party of one.

'A table beside the window, yes? A table here for two.'

'Just one today.'

He gestures for her to sit down and sets the table for

two. He gives her a menu and places another down across from her. The menu is in Greek, with English descriptions below each item. Upon her first visit and perusal of the menu, she noticed several spelling errors in the English version, so she avoids looking at the menu. It makes her want to take a red pen and make corrections.

She waits. The ritual continues. She admonishes herself for not bringing her sketch pad and glares at the man who seems to encapsulate waiter, host and perhaps café owner to entice him to come take her order. After half an hour, he approaches her.

'You are alone?'

'Yes, and I would like to order. Moussaka and a glass of sparkling water.'

She gives him back the menus and his eyes drift to her hands and up her wrists which show long scratch marks stretching up her lower arm. He pauses as she pulls back her hands and places them under the table. He walks away.

On her way back to the cottage she visits the pharmacy. The girl behind the counter says her English is not good. She is correct in that assessment. When Marion pulls up her sleeves to show her arms and says 'rash' followed by a miming motion of scratching, the girl merely examines her arms and says, 'No rash, just itch.'

She leaves with a bottle of calamine lotion and uses it religiously. It does nothing.

When Agnes arrives a few days later, Marion is almost looking forward to seeing the sour woman. She starts to unload on her unsuspecting visitor before she has set down her cleaning supplies and linen.

Marion had always wanted to visit Greece. When she was in love, she suggested to Ernest that they go for their honeymoon. He felt it would be better to buy a house instead. So they bought their cottage in the backside of nowhere. It was the only place they could afford. Ernest promised as things improved, the first thing they would do was buy a house back in Dublin, close to the city centre. In the meantime, when they were both working at the ad agency, they would drive up every morning together discussing art and the projects they were assigned.

She concentrated on the whirl of her pen on the paper in front of her. Now that she looks like a calamity, Agnes can no longer completely ignore her and keeps eyeing her brief expanse of forearms, shins and neck which are angry and raw. The twist in her mouth makes it seem like she wants to put on a surgical mask, which is slightly ironic given her general lack of hygiene.

Marion reminisces on the early stages of her marriage and when she found out she was expecting. She wasn't trying to get pregnant, but she wasn't trying not to either. It seemed like a normal progression and she was excited at the concept of starting a family with Ernest. When Sean came, beautiful and wailing, swaddled in neediness and sleepless nights, she realised that family came at a price. Staying at home with him was the only option. Childcare costs were too high to justify along with the mortgage payment. She thought she could put her dreams on hold until Sean got to primary school. A few years soon turned into eighteen. Her paints dried up along with her ambition. An unfinished painting hung in the kitchen all those years. She left it hanging in the hope that one day she would complete it. Instead, her eyes were always drawn to the canvas when she particularly resented the monotonous activities of child-rearing, taking care of Ernest and managing the house. Bitterness took root deep within and systematically took over every activity in her daily routine.

Every day she felt a little less like herself. She missed her old life. She missed the art and the buzz working with other artists. She missed the city. She blamed Ernest. He loved coming home from work and having his dinner placed before him on the table. He took joy in pottering around in the garden, reading stories with Sean and sitting in his favourite chair in the lounge watching *Who Wants to be a Millionaire?*

In the beginning, she coped. She lived in a cocoon with Sean. Then her son grew up. As he got older, it was obvious that he hated country life. Off he went to university in Dublin. As soon as he got his engineering diploma, he left. He went as far away from her as possible. Marion would sit at the kitchen table waiting in anticipation for his calls from Sydney. They were always brief and stilted, and she'd get off the phone and be so remorseful for instilling the ambition in him to get out and experience the world away from the corner shop and one-street town. Ernest only laughed at her and asked what did she expect?

The door slamming alerts her to Agnes's departure. She is left only with her blank page and thoughts of her past, trying to figure out when it had gone wrong.

She met Ernest in art school. She always knew she would be an artist. From her earliest memories of trying to make the crayon move across the page to replicate the image in her mind. By the time she was a teenager, she had graduated to paint and canvas and perfected the strokes to capture her inner vision. She embraced her matriculation and anticipated with great excitement the start of art school. It was everything she imagined, entire days spent perfecting drawings, learning new techniques and discussing idealistic creative concepts with her peer group who were just as passionate about the subject.

Ernest was in her oil-painting class during her third year of college. He was doing a degree in arts management and decided to take the class as an elective. He was a friendly and talkative fellow. He told her that he was going to work as an art dealer or gallery owner someday. He wanted to get to know the craft in a hands-on manner which was why he was taking the class as an elective. It became apparent early into the term that while he could not paint, he outshone everyone in the art of conversation.

He was so free with his admiration of her work that she felt compelled to help him with his projects. She would sit beside him with paintbrush in hand showing how to make the stokes sweep across the page to create tension and movement or show form and lighting. He would watch her work on his canvas. She fell in love with the way he gazed at her. They shared their first kiss cleaning paintbrushes.

They grew closer as the last year of school approached. They made plans. They would work for a few years in the more lucrative corporate environment and, once they had a nest egg saved, they would open a gallery. She would paint, and Ernest would manage the gallery and a few other promising artists. An advertising agency asked her to interview for a job as an assistant art director. She was offered the job at the end of the first interview. She asked if her boyfriend could interview for the open junior account executive position and was initially met with hesitation. However, they went ahead with the interview and offered him a position as well.

The work was far more enjoyable than she had expected. It was a vibrant environment. She was busy and constantly pushed to come up with images that were innovative. While she wasn't painting, she was drawing and bringing her visions to life, and her boss began to come to her for input on how to create looks for print and video advertisements. It was instant gratification when she saw her work in magazines. She remembers being in love then, but now she wonders if it was with Ernest or her career.

She did not regret her son, but she never wanted any more children. Once Sean was born, she spent her days in the country alone with him. As he grew older, she existed on the periphery of his life as a gloried minder and chauffer, bringing him to school, swim lessons or sports training. She wanted to teach him art, to give herself the opportunity to paint or put pencil to heavy paper stock. But her son was not interested. He just wanted to play, kick a ball around or run wild with the other boys. She tried to get him to play piano—for any form of art would do. He was so surly with his piano teacher that she refused to take him for a second term.

Ernest told her that boys just wanted to be boys, whatever that meant. Never having a brother, she didn't understand. She came to comprehend that it meant they can't sit still in isolation, practising the piano or holding a paintbrush. With that advice dispensed to her, Ernest would go outside and kick the ball to their son as her hope to keep the bond between herself and Sean slowly dissolved until there was no commonality to establish rapport. The piano got dusty and the paint dried up.

There was no art in her life and bitterness bloomed in to hate. She tried to crush it by reaching out to Ernest. She waited for Ernest to come home and find out about the things he was working on. Ernest told her, 'I don't want to talk about work when I am at home with you and Sean. It is stressful. I'd rather leave it all at the office.'

Anger and antagonism consumed her. She was the one with the real talent when they were at school. She was the one with the promising future. Now her days are spent doing laundry, cooking dinner and being overlooked, unrecognised. She is left in the kitchen by herself, scrubbing pots and stewing in her bitterness at night.

She tried not to be angry. She swallowed her displeasure. Instead of going away and allowing her to embrace what had become her life, the feeling festered. Wrath became carefully concealed behind her gritted teeth and saccharine voice. Ernest was oblivious, and Sean lived in different worlds called Australia and his mid-twenties. She felt no love for Ernest—it had been strangled by the hate she secretly harboured for him.

But then a miracle happened. Sonia, a friend from art school, messaged her on Facebook. She spun her life since the advertising agency as taking a break from her career to be more flexible with her family and allowing her time to paint. The lies came easily. Sonia was now the creative director at a publishing house in London specialising in children's books. She said they were always looking for freelance illustrators and she should submit some of her artwork. Sonia remembered her funny doodles. Marion furtively worked on a few pieces and slipped them in the post.

It was a few months before she heard anything, and she had almost forgotten that she had sent her work to the contact person Sonia had given her. At first, she was asked to do a few small, standalone projects for unpublished authors. The requests started to come more regularly and then she received requests for book covers and picture-book series. It was almost a year before she could count on work, but she felt happier, lighter than she had in years.

~

She goes back to the pharmacy few days later and is more forceful with the clerk when she says the word 'rash'. The girl calls into the back in a callous manner and an older man comes out. Marion goes through the same motions with him: 'rash' and then mimics the scratching, this time not quite touching her skin as she is afraid she might not be able to stop rubbing once she starts. He looks at her arms, no longer just dry, flaky and red, but decorated with broken skin and wet blood and he says the same thing.

'No rash. Itch.'

He turns, picks up a tube of cream and hands it to her. She is exasperated but hopeful when she returns home. She looks it up online and sees that it is hydrocortisone. Her confidence is short-lived, as applying the cream only makes her want to scrub it down to her bones.

Now the locals are beginning to annoy her. The pharmacist and his assistant are dismissive when she returns. When she goes to the restaurant, the staff keep tormenting her with the second place setting. They keep pretending that they do not understand her every time she says, 'No one will be joining me today. One place setting only.'

Every day, she tries a new way of saying the same thing.

'I am travelling on my own. I am not meeting anyone.'

'Just one person. I am holidaying on my own.'

'My husband is dead. I am a widow.'

They just nod and smile and say, 'Yes, yes. Very nice day.' And leave the table with the second setting to mock her.

Every day, she waits for the imaginary husband to not show up and this feeds her frustration. Today, she will visit the doctor. She got the name and the address from the indifferent pharmacist the last time she was in to find another solution to her skin irritation.

She never anticipated being sick in Greece. She hadn't seen her own GP for years, even when he approached her at Ernest's funeral to see if she 'needed to talk'. She is apprehensive at best and sceptical at worst. She hopes the local doctor might be able to diagnose her ailment and have enough English to tell her how to alleviate the symptoms. In the meantime, her moussaka appears and the waiter fades into the kitchen. It smells good but looks a little burnt and tastes a lot drier than the one she had two days ago.

Once finished with her lunch, she continues down a road she has never been before, following her rudimentary drawing from the pharmacist. She stops at a newer house, its door containing a profession plaque with a caduceus and a name in Greek below it. She knocks and waits for the door to open. The door swings open and the man who showed her around her holiday cottage stands in front of her. She is confused.

'Are you leaving?' she asks.

He smiles and says, 'No, please come in.'

He looks like he did at their first meeting, wearing dress slacks, a pale blue, fine cotton shirt and brown leather Oxfords.

'I am looking for the doctor. I must have gotten the wrong address.'

'Ah, no. You are in the right place. I am the doctor.'

She wonders if business is so slow in the sleepy village that he moonlights as an estate agent to make ends meet. When her pause becomes awkward, he says, 'The house you have rented, it belongs to my family. I grew up in that house. When I came back here to work as the doctor, I had this house built. It is a better location and bigger. It has more modern conveniences. We rent the other house to tourists during the year, but my mother, she loves that house and we could never sell it while she is alive.'

She nods and tries to think of something to say but the gnawing of her rash makes trivial conversation elusive to her.

'Now, please, come in. Is there something wrong at the house or do you require a doctor?'

'Yes, a doctor. I know I don't have an appointment, but I hope you might be able to see me.'

He slowly walks her through the modest Greek home. They enter what could have been a sitting room. It has been converted into a doctor's surgery. Upon the sideboard lies a tray with medical instruments and beside it a bottle of Ouzo, begging the question of its use. Was it for consumption or disinfection? The examining table is in place of a sofa.

'Of course, Mrs Molloy. There are not many sick people in our village today. What is bothering you?'

'Marion, you can call me Marion. It's a rash. I don't know what is causing it, but it's everywhere. It just keeps getting worse,' she says as she scratches the inside of her wrist. Once she realises what she is doing, she stops with great difficulty.

As she pulls up her sleeves and holds her arms out for the doctor to look. She watches his reaction to the raw skin. She does not imagine his horrified expression as he gingerly touches the flesh and asks her questions. He looks at her neck and her legs, the signs of the insidious ailment on every piece of exposed flesh he sees. He gives her a steroid shot, a prescription for a strong antihistamine that will make her sleepy and the advice to keep it clean and dry. She makes her way back to the village to fill her prescription and get the special soap to wash her tender skin. With her bag of remedies and a renewed sense of purpose, she heads home.

She enjoys the walk to her cottage, down the narrow lane that has seen more goats than cars. The fecundity of summer and its heat has slowed down the growth process of the weeds that line the road by the stone walls. The dust has settled, with the slight dampness of winter rain compressing it into the hard earth track that makes up the lane. A tractor passes, and its engine sounds pathetic. Then she sees him. Sitting up on the seat of the old tractor put-putting along using one hand to steer, is a man. He is rubbing the wrist that is not steering against wheel to the beat of the engine chug. It is Ernest, her husband, whom she had buried five years earlier. She stares and stares until the tractor disappears around the bend. The itch has infiltrated her mind, playing tricks on her.

It is making her crazy and now she is seeing her dead husband. She does not care that he is here in Greece with her. She can only think about how much she wants to scratch the sensation on her neck, that sensitive space in the crease of her arm, behind her knees, where her waistband touches in her middle. Everything reminds her of the pleasure she would get from fingernails on flesh, scraping the irritated skin. The steroid shot does no good and the bathing offers little relief.

~

Over the next few days, she finds herself skipping her visits to the village, living on tea and long-life milk and dry sweet crackers that she bought in the mini-market. She draws with a crazed passion and waits for Agnes to come back. The only time she can forget about her affliction is when she is talking at Agnes. She wonders if farmer Ernest knows Agnes. She speculates the possibility of farmer Ernest being dead Ernest's twin lost at birth. He had no siblings, but that doesn't mean it is not remotely possible. She pictures Agnes as a saint sent to heal her.

Saturday arrives, and when Agnes opens the door, her eyebrows raise and she pauses before she continues into the cottage. The neat and orderly designated art space no longer exists. Papers occupy most of the living area and kitchen. There are bundles of paper on almost every piece of furniture. Ink drawings containing increasingly darker and darker images sit on stacks surrounding Marion, who does not get up but continues creating images at a mad pace. Agnes does not really like to clean, so Marion feels she is doing her a favour by decreasing the surface space Agnes pretends to dust.

Marion starts to rant, she is not sure if it is in her head, or if she is speaking out loud. She spews the story of her spiral from depression and unhappiness to rage and retribution.

It all started when Ernest was laid off, his company downsized. Suddenly, he was home all the time. She told her friends that he was semi-retired and was only doing some freelance work with projects that really took his fancy. He was just at home. Not at home in the ready-to-help-out-at-any-moment kind of way. He did not make her life any easier. He was at home in the I've-got-one-extra-person-to-take-care-of kind of way.

Every time she turned around, he was in her space. 'What shall we have for lunch?' he would say as he watched her folding laundry on the kitchen table.

She'd say, 'I wasn't planning on having lunch. Once I finish up with the laundry and ironing, I am going to get a cup of tea and a banana and work on some sketches for my illustration project.'

'Oh, I thought we would have lunch together now that I am home,' he would tell her. Why would she want to prepare one more meal for them?

She looks up and notices that Agnes is not wearing her earbuds today. She is in the kitchen space flicking toast crumbs from the counter to the floor where they would inevitably be dispersed by feckless sweeping-brush strokes throughout the area.

She would do what Agnes was doing, rushing through her daily chores with no commitment to allow her to spend as much time in her makeshift studio. It was all she looked forward to. It was her redemption. It was a few hours a day that she did not have to think about her mediocre life with everyday chores and what to make for dinner.

The antipathy she had felt back then repeated on her like onions, filling her mouth with a bad taste. The defeated feeling from when she first gave up work had lulled to a weak ebb. Now it returned, becoming much stronger, fortified by annoyance and anger. She wanted companionship twenty years earlier, but Ernest had left her in their narrow-minded village to slowly stifle in an unexceptional life. Now she just wants the solitude to draw for hours without interruption. If he continued to get in her way, she feared her work would become subpar and the editors would look elsewhere, find someone more reliable whose artistic talent was better. Fear and frustration became a blinding rage. He could not take it from her again.

They would have breakfast together and instead of heading off to work, he would stay seated his chair at the kitchen table with his third cup of coffee and the local newspaper, harrumphing, making little belching noises and scratching the inside of his wrist where his eczema was irritated by his watch as he read the entire paper. And there she was, cleaning up, watering the plants, putting the rubbish out and starting a load of laundry. He just sat there, making a production of turning the newspaper pages and occasionally calling out fragments of sports news. She never was a sports person. Art had always been her life's passion. She didn't support a team and certainly didn't give a toss who was now out of the FAI cup.

This continued throughout the day—every day—as she got on with her daily chores. She would have just stopped hoovering, and there was Ernest in the middle of the carpet asking, 'Do you think the clothes have been left on the line too long? The towels will get scratchy if they stay out there much longer, and I think the sun bleaches the colour from them anyway.'

She remembers hating all those little monotonous jobs and took no pride in doing them. Now that Ernest was unemployed, instead of looking for a new job or even a hobby, he took it upon himself to tell her how she could be doing everything better. It was his new calling.

'I noticed you left the chicken out to defrost. Should it be on the counter or would you be better off sticking it in the fridge to save us from getting botulism?' His sarcastic sense of humour had once made her laugh; now it made her want to throttle him. She said nothing.

'I see you are watering the indoor plants every day. Wouldn't it be better to put them outside on the rainy days and save you watering them?'

'How hot do you have the iron? When you are pressing the shirts, surely if you have it a little hotter there will be less wrinkles and you get it done twice as fast?'

Ernest was intent on providing feedback for every task, no matter how small.

By dinner, she could barely look across the table at him much less dredge up enough affection to have a conversation. Even his teeth scraping across the fork depositing the potentially bacteria-infested chicken into his mouth grated on her nerves and made her want to scream. She gripped her fork tight in an effort not to stab him in the eye.

And once dinner was finished, the conversation was inevitable.

'I liked how you did the chicken last week better. It was less dry.'

'Hmmm.'

'What shall we watch tonight. How about *Who Wants to be a Millionaire?* I'll go turn on the telly. Join me when you are ready.'

She hated quiz shows. She cleaned up the dinner and then disappeared to work on her sketches for a new children's book about a monster family. She came down to earth when Ernest popped his head in the door and said, 'What did you get up to? I'm off to bed are you coming?'

~

At this stage, Marion looks down at the page she has been drawing. It is a caricature of the scene she has just played through in her mind. The page is so dark that the ink is beginning to bleed into the back of the paper. This image is more dark than light. She lifts the page and blows lightly, then sets it down in a stack on the dining side of her table. Agnes is giving a wide berth to her and her paper stacks as she pretends to clean.

Now Agnes is putting on rubber gloves and picking up the sheets and towels. Marion finds this hysterical. The only time Agnes does something with clean items, is the time she feels the need to wear the Marigolds.

Now Marion is scratching enthusiastically. She realises that she has not changed out of her pyjamas and they are bloody. The blood is not beautiful and fascinating the way Ernest's blood looked. It is red and slightly brownish in areas, caked and without the vibrant depth of hue.

When Agnes comes out of the bedroom with bloodied bed sheets and towels, Marion tells the illustration, 'I couldn't help it, really. He was offering to help me with art. Him, help me! I was the one with so much talent!'

She is calm then and looks up to see that Agnes is gone. So is the desire to scratch her skin. She looks down at her hands. How ironic that the only place the itching has avoided is the area underneath the rings on her finger. The red, weeping skin decorates the tops of her hands to her fingernails. She thinks if it could delve under her short, square nails, it would be there too. But there is a pristine band of white, unmarred skin underneath her rings if she examines her hands closely. She wonders why this is. If she believed in magic or God she might think that Ernest is sending her a message. She only knows she won't take off her rings because it is the last stronghold of unspoiled skin on her body. And she likes to think there is a last vestige of purity in her.

There is a rap on the door and words shouted from outside. Has she been there minutes, hours or days? In this alternative world of insanity, there is a different clock.

Marion stays in her seat and Agnes enters. She rushes through the door, pauses to hone in on her target, then points with strong thrusting strokes and far greater enthusiasm than she ever used for cleaning. Behind her trudge two Greek policemen observing the chaos of drawings decorating every surface of the room. They look with a morbid curiosity at the content of the illustrations.

'There she is, the woman I was telling you about. Murderer! She told me she killed her husband. Evil woman! You must take her away!' Agnes is screaming, her voice shrill and containing what Marion thinks is a faintly English accent. The pitch of her voice and the way the English words are coordinated make Marion believe she is not originally Greek, as she had thought, but possibly from her own native land. Marion recognises something else akin to herself five years ago. It is wrath, anger wrapped up in hate, seasoned with bitterness and covered in resentment. Marion thinks that the salve easing the agony of the prevailing itch might be an emotion she has not been acquainted with for some time. It is compassion.

Blood, both fresh and dried, colour her fingernails and embed in the cuticles of the hands she holds out. She wants them to take her. One of the men is on his mobile phone, and she thinks she hears the word 'doctor'. She is rises from her seat slowly and walks toward the police, ready to go to where ever they will take her. She does not care about the blood that seeps from her skin and stains her clothes. She just appreciates the itching has stopped. In its place is relief. She is light-headed with the feeling. The officers back away from her as if she is contagious.

There is a rapid fire of Greek from one of the officers to Agnes and she replies, equally fast and sharp. Agnes looks annoyed and shifty. Nobody says anything. Marion is ready.

'She's right. I murdered my husband. I did. Please take

me!'

There is the sound of footsteps clipping quickly up the path to the front door. Once again, the doctor frames the doorway as he did when Marion first arrived. This time it is in an effort to spring in to the house rather than propel himself out from it.

'It is fine. The rash, the itch, it's gone. I don't need a doctor anymore. I did it. I killed my husband and, now that you know, Ernest will stop. He will make it go away.'

She laughs as the mania takes over where rage once resided. She is liberated from both her brain and her body as she collapses in front of the surprised policemen.

~

The doctor looks at Marion and then reproachfully at Agnes. He shakes his head vigorously as if trying to dislodge what he now comprehends. No steroid would have helped relieve Marion's irritation. Agnes, this woman, his mother, has been poisoning Marion, probably by washing her sheets and towels in the oleander plant that decorates the countryside. This is not her first effort to make a tenant evacuate their old home, but it is certainly the most effective.

'Mama, not again! Why? Why must you do this?'

~

It is weeks later, and Marion still wonders what Agnes is doing. The room is not how she would have imagined a jail cell. To her, it is paradise. There are no bars, just four walls. There is no sunlight, as there are no windows. She has mixed feelings about this feature. On one hand, there is no natural lighting to give shading to the walls, which are the colour of a stretched canvas. On the other hand, it offers her a greater expanse to showcase her talent.

Nobody bothers her here. At first, she thought it was because they did not speak English. As different officers and doctors came she realised that the Greeks had very good English. She plays with the idea that they do not want to develop any emotional ties as she will be sent back to Ireland once the paperwork is complete. She wanders around the room eyeing the beauty. She understands now that they have left her in peace to focus on the art. Ernest gave her the idea and Agnes's poisoning provided her the weeping skin to access the medium. This is not a box but an opportunity.

She scratches her arms that no longer itch but have not healed because she will not allow it. No matter how many times they try to bandage her limbs, there is always a place to let the red liquid beautiful flow and give her fingers the paint to create her masterpiece decorating the walls.

Biographies

Adrian Taheny has appeared in many notable theatre productions, including Druid's Threepenny Opera. Now retired from the Irish financial services industry, he pursues his passion for writing and photography. He had two stories published in Storytellers: New Writing from Ireland as well as having had several of his poems published and recorded. He is in the process of completing his first novel.

Alix Moore is a Londoner who followed her heart to Ireland in 2016. She studied piano and voice at the Guildhall School of Music. She is currently working on her first novel – a psychological thriller set in the world of music and medicine. Her short story, 'The Surprise', was published in Storytellers: New Writing from Ireland.

Caroline Bale, from Blackrock in County Dublin, writes crime fiction with a psychological twist, drawing upon her practice as a psychotherapist to create complex plots and engaging characters. Remember Me, her crime fiction novel set in York, was selected as a finalist in the Irish Writers Centre Novel Fair 2018.

Jenny Wright was born in Edinburgh and lives in Dublin. Her short story, 'Frankie', was included in All Good Things Begin, an anthology of new writing. Jenny's novel for children, The Cinderella Project, was published in 2018.

Mark Bastow's first two fantasy adventure novels are set in seventeenth century London. His third novel, Crying into Hoo Hole, concerns policing in Yorkshire and he is currently working on a novel of corporate intrigue. Short stories include supernatural, crime and historical fiction, as well as tales written for children.

Martin Keating's fiction has been long and shortlisted for the Fish Short Story Prize, the Seán Ó Faoláin International Short Story Prize, and the Bryan McMahon Short Story Award. In 2016, his story, 'The Welfare Visitor', included in this collection, won the Dalkey Creates Short Story Prize. Moriarty, his historical crime novel set in Edwardian Dublin, was shortlisted for the Irish Writers Centre 2018 Novel Fair.

Susan Rodgers worked as a freelance writer and editor for magazines in the United States before moving to Ireland in 2001. Her short story, 'The Other Woman', was published in Storytellers: New Writing from Ireland and she is in the process of completing an anthology of short stories entitled Body on the Beach.

Ferdia Mac Anna (Editor) is a novelist, director of film and TV drama, screenwriter and lecturer. He produced a BAFTA-winning BBC/RTE drama series, Custer's Last Stand-Up (2000-2002). His novel, The Last of the High Kings was made into a Hollywood movie starring Jared Leto, Gabriel Byrne and Christina Ricci. He has taught at UCD, DCU, NUI Maynooth, American College Dublin and The Open University. His debut feature film, All About Eva, was selected for the Dublin International Film Festival (2015)